Devil's
Doorway

By Sue York

Sue York

Cover Design by Shannon Johnson, Baraboo, WI

Author Photograph by Brotcke Photography, Payette, ID

ACKNOWLEDGEMENTS

My first debt of gratitude goes to my husband, Roger, who has heard me talk about this book forever over the years. Without your support I may have given up on this story. I love you.

My children, Josh, Courtney, Lauren, and Dakota for going with me to the lake for research and hearing endlessly about "the book". Especially Dakota for hiking the bluffs with me in hopes we would find that old step on the West Bluff.

To my friend, Michelle Dent for giving me insight on what it was like working at the North Shore Chateau in high school.

To my friends Aimee Schulz and Marlie Ernst who didn't know they were characters in a fiction book.

To Shannon Johnson for creating a beautiful cover for this book (To whom I owe a beer . . . or two or three).

To Susan Johansen, Naturalist at Devil's Lake State Park, for answering all my questions, helping me with some research for pictures, and guiding me on places I didn't know about.

And finally, to my editor Cara Lockwood, who kept encouraging me to finish this book and to adhere to her suggestions that I change the names within to fit the place. They fit like a glove.

Chapter One

My friends and I have plans to spend our days on the beach and hiking all the trails. We've heard the rumors about what happened in the lake back when the town was first settled, but we don't really believe any of it.

The rumor is that a curse had been quiet until the late 1800s when everyone in Gem City vanished without a trace. Some say the curse was cast by an angry Illinois tourist and it presented itself in the form of a unique rock formation out in the water, different size rocks that were stacked on top of each other and each one slightly tilted to keep the balance. Four of them were visible when Gem City residents disappeared.

Besides, getting tan, scoping out the boys, working at the chateau and staying late for the dances will be the only things on our mind for the next few months. History is not something we care about.

Today the air is flat, sticky and looks to be a "stay cool and indoors" kind of day, but Lena won't have it. Lena loves the lake and makes us all hike those trails with her every week.

Lena, Hannah, Nicola and I know the trails in and out and how far to each bluff and how long it takes to hike them. It never gets boring seeing all that beauty in one place . . .

After several phone calls and patiently waiting for Lena, we finally head out to the lake and have decided that today we will hike the bluff to the east and then swim the rest of the afternoon.

"Water bottles?" Lena asks, checking to make sure hers is in her backpack. Lena stands five-foot-four and wears her brown hair short. Lena and I have been friends since the second grade when she first moved to town.

"Check!" the rest of us say.

"Hats?" Lena glances round at the group, assessing each one's attire.

"Check!"

"Walking sticks?"

Hannah rolls her green eyes, pushing her shoulder-length brown hair out of her face.

"Funny, Lena! You know we don't have walking sticks." Hannah and I became friends in the ninth grade, playing together in the clarinet section of the band.

Hannah always makes fun of the way Lena creates lists and double checks everything before we head out. But Lena is only trying to be careful and make sure we are well prepared.

Lena probably keeps a first aid kit along with a flare. At least she plans well. I know she carries binoculars for good measure. We must be sure we can still scope out the boys from above.

"Let's go, guys!" Nicola can't wait to start hiking. She's the go-getter in the group and wears her long blonde hair up in a peppy ponytail. Nicola and I shared the same gym class in seventh grade five years ago and have been friends ever since.

No matter how much we whine to Lena about the heat and humidity, we still enjoy the hikes. We always find something new.

"So, Lena, are we taking the easy trail this time?" I ask, hoping that with the humidity and heat we will take a smooth hike to the top rather than a steep incline that will have sweat rolling off our backs the whole way up. At least today we are all wearing jean shorts, tank tops and tennis shoes to keep somewhat cool.

"Rin, if you have to ask then you do not know me at all." Lena heads to the front of the group. "You know we never take the easy trail up."

I figure she would say that. Keeping my complaints to myself, I fall into the back of the line as we make our way to the start of Potholes Trail. It is without a doubt, the most difficult of all the trails.

The trail practically goes straight up. The bluffs rise five hundred feet high and we go all the way to the top. However, the view is divine and well worth the agony.

Lena must park at the lot furthest away from the bluff. She purposely avoids any spots closer. Adds to our hike, she always says.

"Now, here we are at the crossroads. Grottos Trail to our left, which leads to Balanced Rock Trail and to our right, that leads to Potholes Trail. Which one will lead us to the trail we will be hiking today?" Nicola stands there, pointing in each direction.

"Crossroads? Really. More like a fork," Lena argues.

"Does it really matter? Do we really have to stop and check the trail map every time? We know the way," I point out.

"Yes, we do," Hannah chimes in, pushing her long brown hair out of her eyes. "It's like a weekly tradition."

"Come on, guys. Let's get hiking!" Nicola says, jumping up and down being her usual, childlike antsy self and making us all laugh.

Walking on the loose scree feels like broken stoneware beneath our feet. We all grow silent since the noise is so loud. Hannah stops flat.

"What are you stopping for?" I demand to know now that my nose has been flattened into her back.

"Look," she says, pointing down a small path to the left. "I never noticed that before."

"What are we stopping for?" Lena asks, impatiently tapping her foot on the scree.

"Look!" I point to the concrete step slap just off the main path.

"That's always been there. Let's get going." Lena anxiously continues walking.

"Well, we haven't seen it before," the three of us say at the same time.

Lena is no longer listening, as she's walking off through the canopy of trees toward Potholes Trail. Above us, the birds chirp away to each other. The heat and humidity don't feel too terrible here beneath their shade. Looking ahead down the path, it looks quite eerie, with the trees providing a dark canopy above us and throwing shadowy figures in the wind.

As usual, we take the left route along the trees. It appears we are walking forever before we find yet another fork right is the CCC Trail and left is Grottos

Trail edge of the bluff, eyeing the rocks that just sit there, daring to be climbed.

We don't, of course. There have been too many injured rock climbers at the lake. We stick to the path that seems to have been here forever. And all the green of the trees and plant life hide the only signs of the fall season of dead leaves, covering the ground of these beautiful woods.

"Look, look!" Nicola runs to the last fork on this path. "We made it," she exclaims as though this were our first time here.

"Let's take a brief rest before we go up," Lena says.

I always wondered why we took the harder way up. We seem to walk a quarter of a mile or more from the parking lot to where the actual trail begins. Right past the store, the canoes, and the picnic areas and beach. Why not just take the lower trail, just once?

"Rest time is over," Lena commands. She would probably make a great drill sergeant, though I keep that thought to myself.

We continue up the east bluff as each of us is panting away with the change in elevation. This trail is one of the shortest at the lake but is a difficult trail to hike and takes about two hours to hike from the bottom to the top.

"Have to rest. Can't breathe!" We are not even an eighth of the way up the worst trail and I swear I am going to die.

"Okay, one more rest." Lena gasps while trying to breathe. The humidity and heat are finally getting to her. All I can think is that it's about time. The first rest we took was not long enough. She will make sure that this is the last until we reach the top.

The rocks that form each step all the way up are quartzite and they are quite smooth and very cool to the touch, even with the weather being so extreme.

All you want to do is press your face against their coolness for a brief relief from the heat. Rocks are slippery as well. You must watch your step, so you don't fall. That would not be pretty.

"This trail never gets old. Look at the way it just goes right between that wall of rocks. Just enough space for someone to walk through," Hannah chatters on. "It's as if the large rock on this trail split in two."

The steps go right up through this split and as I look, it seems as though I could put it back together like a puzzle. A treasure, I am sure, that many just pass through without much thought. I, for one, stop and view everything as if it were the first time.

"Rin, are you coming? We are almost to the top." Lena tries not to be snappy. She doesn't want to start an argument. She and I tend to do that quite a bit on these hikes.

"Yes, yes. Sorry I was lost in thought," I venture so we can keep moving.

"I thought we would never make it to the top," Hannah lets out while trying to catch her breath.

"I am with you," Nicola adds.

We take a very quick stop at the top to catch our breath even though it feels like my pounding heart will jump right out of my chest. I'm so wet from sweat, it feels like I just came out of the lake from swimming.

Once at the top, it's not flat as some people would think. There are still rocks and hills covered in beautiful trees and flowers as the trail continues to the right and the left. We take the left so we may get to our destination and favorite picnic spot.

Finally, we arrive at Devils Doorway. We can see all the way across the lake from here. The parking lot, beach and store stand in the distance.

The view takes my breath away in minutes. To the east, the view goes on for miles and the river is just beyond. Looking to the south, another bluff stares back at me. There are no trails that I know of on the South Bluff.

Devils Doorway is just as its name suggests. Quartzite rock has stood for hundreds of years in the shape of a door, which is three and a half feet wide and twenty-five feet high.

"This view never gets old," I quietly share.

"And you wanted to take the lower trail, Rin," Lena says smugly.

"Enough!" Hannah says. "Let's enjoy our lunch here and relax a bit."

Choosing the flattest rock, Hannah and Nicola lay out our lunch. I am still taking in the view, snapping a few pictures as though I have never been here before.

I catch Nicola and Hannah making faces at each other as they sit and chatter. *These pictures will be great blackmail should I need it,* I think to myself with an evil smile.

"What are you smiling about?" Lena demands to know.

"Oh, Lena, will you relax? A person *can* smile without rhyme or reason you know." I smirk at her making my way to our blanket for lunch and mindless chatter. Lunch is our favorite turkey subs from the local Subway and, of course, chips and water. We never drink soda when we are out hiking.

"So, who is going up into the doorway first?" Nicola says excitedly as we fold up our blanket and store what is left of our lunch back into our backpacks. The hardest part of Devils Doorway is climbing up to it so one can walk through.

It's at least six to eight feet up on another rock. So, in this heat, climbing makes you sweat more all the while the coolness of the rock begs you to plaster your face to it.

"I guess, Nicola, you may as well go up first and then help up the next," Lena says.

"Of course, one of us will have to help her up there," I point out. "This is a group effort."

Not many people take the time to climb up into the doorway because of the difficulty of getting up there, not to mention the challenge of getting back down.

Placing my foot in the small crevice, I straddle the opening and with a hopping motion, I sway all my weight toward the doorway. My whole body is shaking as I lean in toward the rock and try to keep my balance at the same time. Slowly, I take my left hand and reach for a rock higher up to grab while raising my right foot to another crevice.

"Gotcha," Lena says as she takes my left hand in hers and I swing my whole body to the left, catching my feet on the rock in a rock climber's stance. Lena catches

my right hand just before I lose my balance and end up

with a huge scrape on my knee.

"One last pull and you're up," Lena grunts to me

as if I weigh a ton. Catching my breath, I stand up and

start to walk to the other side of the doorway.

Chapter Two

The arguing just never quits here as I wake up from a dead sleep to my mom and Marie fighting once again. I can only imagine what the argument is about this time. Can't I have just one peaceful morning like when I was younger? Thank goodness we live out in the country and do not have neighbors.

Booting up the computer in the family room, I decide to do some research online about the lake. I wondered how we had never seen that concrete step slab before. It seemingly appeared from nowhere.

"How long you going to be on that computer?" Mom yells at me from the doorway.

"I just booted it up. I won't be too long," I say quickly and quietly thinking there is no reason to yell at me since I just rolled out of bed.

"Well, hurry up. I have some bills to pay and I don't have all day. Don't you have work today?" she barks back at me like it's my fault she is in a bad mood. Probably was Lea that caused the fight with Mom and Marie and the rest of us receive the brunt of it.

"Yes, I do. Hannah will be here in an hour to pick me up," I answer looking back at the computer screen. My search doesn't tell me anything about that concrete slab and I am forced to leave it for now.

Hannah arrives to pick me up for work and I am waiting outside for her. I must have called her a million times to see if she was on her way from town to get me. We stop and pick up Lena and head up to Nicola's house behind the high school before we head off to the lake for work. We work noon to six today.

We arrive at the North Shore entrance along Warner Road, the canopy of trees above sing with relaxation and we always drive this road at the speed limit or less to allow enough time to take in the beauty of the quartzite rock on the right and the view of one of the campsites down in the valley to the left.

Nicola, Hannah and Lena chatter quietly about having to listen to "Call Me Maybe," all night from the jukebox.

"Rin! Are you still with us?" Lena asks, again. She's already asked me at least twice before.

"What? Yes, I am still here just enjoying the scenery."

"You see this every day," Hannah points out. "Nothing changes."

"Hannah, you would be surprised as to what will change from day to day." I'm grateful for the opportunity to have lived in the most beautiful place in all of Wisconsin.

I tune them out again as we make our way around yet another bend. To the left is the Nature Center. If you want to know about insects, plant life and such at the lake, they know everything. Me? I don't need lessons. I can learn about the state bird, the mighty mosquito, each time he lands on me and I smash his brains. I laugh to myself. The mosquito isn't the official state bird, but it might as well be. We have more around here than American robins.

"What's so funny back there?" Nicola wants to know.

"Oh, nothing," I say, knowing Nicola wouldn't appreciate a joke that doesn't have to do with boys or Lena who is like a drill sergeant most of the time.

The view to the right as we drive around the curves heading down toward the lake takes my breath away. The trees, as they descend along the hill, are beautiful.

Reaching the bottom, I see the lake in full view and to the right there's plenty of picnic space and a beautiful beach that goes from the Chateau to the end of the West Bluff.

"Thank goodness we have a season sticker and do not have to sit in that long line to get one." Lena points out the window at all the tourists who wait their turn.

We always park near the ticket office and then walk the path to the Chateau for work. We usually arrive early to check out how busy the lake is with tourists so we know how busy an afternoon we may have.

"There, a group of some nice eye candy!" Nicola points and jumps around. We all bust out laughing while we try to get her to quiet down and at least stop jumping up and down. Hopefully, those boys didn't notice. Nicola doesn't care if she embarrasses us all.

The Chateau is known for its Big Band dances on Saturday nights roaring with jazz and swing. The dances have been going since the thirties and forties. And the teens who swarmed them then still come today, older and wiser, wearing their fancy dancing shoes, determined to whoop it up and relive their younger years.

I enjoy working those dances. Lena, Hannah and Nicola never seem to complain either, but Wednesdays are our favorites, mostly because we do not have to work them and can enjoy the fun and the DJ.

Hannah works the gift shop part of the Chateau. She seems to have a knack for getting the souvenirs sold to just about every visitor. She folds the T-shirts just as the boss likes them and her inventory is always spot on. Not to mention, Hannah's amazing with clean up.

Now matter-of-fact Lena works the snack area, perfect for her drill sergeant persona, which helps her make sure inventory and cleanup is done.

At the snack area, Lena sells brats, hotdogs, candy, soda, beer and much more. Of course, there is a college boy named Nate who helps Lena in the snack area, as she isn't old enough to sell alcohol. Surprising, though, the poor boy meekly takes orders from Lena as well. It's kind of funny to watch.

Now Nicola takes care of all the rentals out at the rental shack. The rental shack is just a small porch off the northwest end of the Chateau. Nicola pulls all the equipment out from the basement storage such as the canoes and oars and the life jackets. She sets up all the boats and canoes so customers can easily get them out on the lake.

For Nicola, this is the perfect job for her. Our boss decided that she was too antsy to be inside working the snack area. Keeping her outside where she stays busy continuously suits her.

As for me, I work out in the ice cream shop with another college boy named Kip. We sell ice cream, nachos, popcorn and soda. It's easy but we keep busy cleaning when not helping customers.

"Okay, let's make sure we all get done and out of here on time tonight," Lena commands like a drill sergeant.

"Yeah, yeah we know," I say. We all know how Lena's night will go and are grateful to not have to work in the same proximity with her.

It's Wednesday night, a dance, and that is why Lena wants to get out of here quickly so she can relax. Dance starts at eight-thirty and we are always done with time to spare. Normally, we don't work on Wednesdays, but our boss asked if we would cover a few hours.

Chapter Three

I relax during my fifteen-minute break sitting at a picnic table toward the west end of the lake. It's a much-needed break from everyone. Oh, I enjoy time with my friends but when alone, I like the quiet content feeling the lake provides if I sit long enough to hear it.

Even Lena, Nicola and Hannah don't have an actual clue as to how my home life really is. I don't share much.

Chaos reigns at my home daily: everyone fights. My mom fights with my older sister over stupid stuff and when they're not yelling at each other, my parents bicker constantly.

My sister, Lea, just seems to attract trouble. When my parents found out she was sneaking out of her bedroom window do you know what my dad did? No guesses? He nailed the window shut — literally.

From my personal experience, sneaking out of the house via the front door or basement door to the garage never worked. I could shut the door as quiet as possible and somehow the door still seemed to shake the entire house and that would wake up good ole Mom and Dad and I was busted.

The trick, if I was just going outside late at night to chat someone up in the driveway, was to leave the door open a crack and no one knew. I used to do this when my boyfriend stopped over every night after work and I would go out to see him. But Lea never learned what I knew. While I tried to sneak around my parents, Lea seemed to not even care if they found out, seemed to relish the fights she had with Mom. I think Lea just craves attention. Why else do stupid things and get caught? I never want to involve myself in the mess but prefer it to go away. Oh well, back to work I go. Taking in one last deep breath of fresh air, I head back to the ice cream shop.

"Hey, Nicola, how are the rentals today?" I ask on my way back to the ice cream shop.

"Oh, my gosh! I have seen some very nice-looking eye candy today," Nicola exclaims, excited that she saw Treyton as well. "Has definitely made my day." Nicola just knows how to make your day. Her obsession with boys is a constant, like the sun rising in the east.

"Good." I gasp even though that wasn't an answer to my question and continue to the ice cream shop.

"Kip, everything okay while I was gone?" I ask, as he tends to doodle and diddle a lot if not watched closely.

"You know it, dude," Kip says in his surfer style attitude.

Kip is fun to work with. His carefree attitude keeps things smooth and relaxing. Kip has a small dimple on his right cheek, black hair that sweeps in front of his eyes, but he keeps it short in the back. Kip and I are just co-workers and we work well together.

"Well, Kip, go ahead and take fifteen. I think I can manage." Kip is half-way out the door before I get all the words out. I wonder what he does on his breaks. My thoughts are lost as work calls for someone wanting a bag of popcorn and a cherry Icee.

****

Kip is back and we start our clean up. We have to close the ice cream shop early so we can help with cleaning in the Chateau. If I know Lena, Nate hasn't taken his fifteen-minute break and I am sure by now the poor guy needs it.

"All right, Kip, let's head over to the Chateau. You help Hannah and I will pick up where Nate is so he can get his break," I tell him as I pull our deposit from the now balanced cash drawer to drop in the safe.

"Dude, you know it." Kip and I enter the Chateau and there's Nate putting the soft serve machine back together.

"Nate, what does Lena have you doing next?" I ask him to help his nerves.

"Oh, hey Rin, I am supposed to wipe down all the tables and chairs. Then we have the cash drawer and sweeping left," Nate quietly shares so drill sergeant Lena doesn't hear.

"You finish that up and then go take your fifteen and I will grab the soap bucket and wipe down everything that needs to be wiped." Nate looks relieved and stammers a "T-thank you."

Giving pity to Nate, if I work it right, by the time he returns all that will be left to do is the cash drawer. Kip and Hannah usually get done quickly and then take to the sweeping.

For Wednesday night dances, popcorn, candy and soda are sold. The floor doesn't get its usual massive polish like for the Saturday dances, but it does get a good sweeping.

"What a great afternoon." Antsy pants Nicola enters through the back door with her cash bag. "I am telling you; I saw some very nice eye candy from my perch out there today."

Somehow, Nicola manages to get a lot of rentals rented out and still has time to see all the hottest looking guys at the lake. It's like she has radar for eye candy. How she can multitask like that, we will never know.

"Gift shop is a wrap and restocked. Sweeping is done. Let's count some moola and call it a day," Hannah volunteers just as Nate is back from his break. Thankfully, Lena is so busy, she didn't notice he was gone.

We drop our deposit just as the next crew takes out their cash bags. "See you guys in a bit." As the four of us head out the door. We head down to the now deserted beach to sit, relax and get ready for the dance.

"The dance is starting. Should we go?" Nicola whispers.

"Let's just wait a few minutes yet. Let all the eye candy arrive and get their tables and drinks before we go in and start checking them out." Hannah finishes taking her shoes off, digging her toes into the sand.

"How do I talk to Lena?" Nate says so quietly I didn't even hear him walk up behind me.

"Just go up and talk to her. She doesn't bite," I tell him, pointing to Lena as she walks along the beach barefooted.

I sit down in the sand watching Nate walk sheepishly towards Lena. Leaning back on my elbows, I close my eyes and enjoy the fresh breeze blowing off the lake.

"Okay, let's go in. I have had enough of the sand for now." Nicola brushes the sand off her feet and slips them back into her shoes.

"What about Lena?" Hannah asks, putting her shoes back on.

"Leave her. Nate is with her and will make sure she comes into the dance," I answer as I wait for the two of them to leave taking my time to sit up and put my shoes back on.

Ah, the dance. The DJ never disappoints, especially playing mostly fast songs rather than slow songs. Not too many slow dances probably because no one knows anyone. Of course, there's the disco ball of the seventies coming to life which will probably be here for another fifty years and the music bouncing off the walls making the windows dance.

"This is a usual scene, boys on one side and girls on the other," Hannah says matter-of-factly. She cracks us up. We never know when she is going to surprise us like that.

"So, let's just request an awesome song and get out there and shake it till we drop!" Nicola pipes in.

"Okay, so what song do we want to hear?" I ask, knowing what I would request.

"I am thinking maybe a little 'Dangerous and Cyclone,'" Hannah tosses in.

"Oh, and how about 'Gotta Get Me Some,'" I say, perfect music in my opinion to start out the night.

"All right, Nicola, you go put in the requests and let's dance!" Lena says eagerly.

The four of us take our place on the dance floor and move with the music and pray there isn't a slow song coming up next. Nicola wouldn't mind a slow dance with Treyton but the rest of us just prefer to let loose and dance.

"A slow song! Just great, nothing like being a wall flower," I say as I begin to move to the closest wall just as someone grabs my hand and pulls me back to the dance floor.

"Kip, I thought you went home?" I notice that he is completely drenched.

"Nah, I like to swim in the evening before heading home and tonight I thought I would hang out here." We sway back and forth to the music. I look around and there is Lena dancing with Nate, Nicola dancing with Treyton as expected and Hannah.

"Where is Hannah?" I whisper to myself as the song comes to the end and I thank Kip for the dance. I find Lena and Nicola to see if they have seen Hannah.

"I haven't seen her," Nicola says as she walks to the refreshment counter with Treyton.

"I saw her walk outside just as we hit the dance floor," Lena replies, trying not to be cute with Nate.

"I will go outside and see if I can find her. The dance will be over soon, and I hope she is okay."

" Oh my gosh! I will feel the pain from this night for a week. My feet are killing me," I groan as I walk outside and find Hannah sitting on a picnic table rubbing her own feet. Lena and Nicola appear next to me just as the last song plays.

"Rin, stop being so dramatic. At least people danced for a change, even some of the boys." Hannah doesn't seem to feel any pain and I am most definitely not being dramatic.

"I agree," Lena says as we walk the path toward Hannah's car to head home. "The songs just kept rolling out and everyone had a great time."

Nicola is quiet for a change. "She is probably still in dreamland from dancing with Treyton all night." Hannah smirks.

"If she only realized that he goes to our school, works the South Shore Store and has been ogling her for a long time," Lena shares matter-of-factly as if she has kept some big secret.

Chapter Four

We manage to get Thursday off, and we decide to not hike or even hang out together. Even the best of friends needs a break. I love the lake, so that is where I am headed for the day. Marie, my older sister, is letting me use her car today while she sleeps. The peacefulness of the lake early in the morning is divine. I could live here. There are four cottages still here at the lake and they sit along the base of the West Bluff.

Back in the early 1900s, the lake became a state park so any other cottages that may have been here then were torn down except those four. Somehow, they managed to work out a deal with the state. Apparently, they are passed down family lines. I wish I was in one of those family lines. I would move out here and never leave.

My first trip to the lake that I can remember was when I was about eight. It was a Sunday and there was a family reunion taking place at the lake on the South Shore. All six of us loaded up the car and headed out. I felt small compared to the bluffs. To me they looked like mountains and I kept calling them mountains until mom explained that they were bluffs and that mountains were much larger in size.

It wasn't until I was in my early teens that I realized how special the lake was to me. If I had a problem or argument with someone, I could just feel at peace among the lake and its quiet spirits talking to me.

Snapping back to reality, I hear sounds of human life amidst the wildlife and the water lapping the beach.

So, it seems some have beat me here. Some kayakers are making their way around the lake. I personally have never done that although it would be neat to at least try it once.

"Well, look who it is." I hear a familiar voice hollering out to me. I turn, it's Lena, Nicola and Hannah.

"You guys get a group rate to show up here?" I laugh as I yell back and glad to see them.

"We figured you would be here, so we decided to join you on our 'alone' day," Hannah chimes in.

"It's quiet out here this early," Lena says as she chooses a spot at the picnic table next to me.

"That's why I love it this early," I share in almost a whisper. The four of us sit there listening to the sounds the lake makes at six o'clock in the morning. It's almost hard for Nicola to keep quiet, but somehow, she is managing quite nicely.

It will be a scorcher in a couple hours. Humidity hits and pretty much makes the day unbearable unless you are in the water. The thought crosses my mind and I know we are all prepared to hike or swim or both. I am content to sit here for now and as it seems, so is everyone else.

Hannah and Nicola decide to walk along the water while Lena and I sit and relax.

"So, Rin, how come you are out here so early?" Lena is direct but not demanding in her curiousness.

"I enjoy it out here this early. Marie was going to bed, so she let me use her car. It's not tense here like at home," I share with her as I know she will understand.

"Gosh, I should do this more often. It's nice and you are right, it's not tense here."

I have tried to get my friends to enjoy the lake with me like this. The relaxing and peacefulness of the lake makes one appreciate the little things in life.

Bouncing back to the table, Hannah and Nicola are all relaxed out and want to hike.

"All right," I tell them. "As long as we are on the South Shore then it's the east bluff we shall hike."

This time, no complaining, no stopping to check the trail map, we all seem more reserved today or maybe we just don't want the arguing. I'm grateful for the quiet to enjoy the serene beauty of the lake.

Arriving at the base of Potholes Trail, we stop and rest for a few.

"I am glad we all met up this morning," Lena whispers quietly.

"Me too," I share. "Lena, why are you whispering?" Laughing out loud, she shrugs her shoulders.

"I don't know." Lena keeps laughing. Her laughter is contagious as we all laugh with her.

"Let's go," Lena commands. She is starting to sound like her old self. We start up the trail and each of us enjoying the cool weather before the humidity strikes. We pass through the puzzle piece once again only to reach "the bowls" as we call them. They are more like potholes within the rock. They are to the left as we hike up the trail. They tend to stay filled with water from the rain and are quite smooth to the touch.

Finally, at the top, we go our usual way to the left to reach the doorway. The right trail leads down the bluff to the group camp area.

As we walk our usual path, I see some of the lake through the trees and to the right are woods with trails that go back to the access road, where a creek runs. There, you can hike down the East Bluff to the North Shore.

"We don't have any lunch," Hannah whines, interrupting my thoughts of the trails through the woods.

"Oh, now don't start. We will have time to get lunch before we go swimming," Lena drills out.

"Phew, we were worried there for a bit." Nicola runs her arm across her forehead trying to wipe the sweat off her that isn't there. We all laugh at this.

"Let's sit up in the doorway again," I add, grateful that we are the only ones here at the doorway for a change. "Hey look at this." I say as I pick up a piece of cloth that looks quite aged.

"What is that?" Lena asks. "It looks old."

"It looks aged and is quite rough for a piece of ordinary cloth." I try my best to explain this piece of cloth while running my fingers over it. I hand it to Lena, and she passes it onto Hannah and lastly Nicola.

"You're right, it's quite rough like it has been out here for years," Hannah agrees with me.

"I think I will keep it," I decide as we begin our climb up into the doorway. The four of us sit there looking out over the lake from the west side of the doorway.

"Great view up here." Lena takes a deep breath and seems to be enjoying the quiet.

"I'm hungry!" Nicola hollers out.

"Really! No warning you just holler that out while it's all quiet and scare us half to death!" I yell.

"Well, I am hungry."

"Me, too," Hannah adds.

"Let's go and see if the South Shore store is open yet and grab a hotdog," Lena says to keep the peace.

"Sounds good," I say, thinking that the south shore store better be open.

We all climb down and take the trail to the left to Balanced Rock Trail for a different view. We reach the bottom and head to the store. It is open and once inside we order hotdogs, chips and water before heading off to our beach.

Chapter Five

Waking again from the continuous arguing from upstairs, I am wishing there was a shower downstairs near my room. But, no, I have to creep quietly upstairs, dash past the kitchen to the bathroom to avoid being dragged into another argument with my mom and sister Marie.

Really? Just one quiet morning, is that too much to ask?

"A quick shower then I am off to Lena's," I plan out loud. "Dad is lucky to be gone so early. He misses all the 'good' stuff. Maybe I should get moving that early."

Most of the arguing seems to happen early because my sister Marie comes in from work about seven-fifteen as Mom is up because of our little brother, Matt, and Marie is heading to bed after working all night.

Heading back to my room, I look outside and see it's raining.

"Well, now I will have to either walk in the rain or call Hannah and see if she is ready to go." Turning my radio on, I crank it up to drown out the arguing. It won't be long, and Marie will be down to chew me out because she needs to sleep.

"Hey, Rin, what's up?" Hannah whispers into the phone.

"Can you pick me up? I was going to walk to Lena's, but its pouring and I have to get out of here," I beg.

"Sure, give me a couple minutes to finish pulling myself together, get my chores done and I will be out to get ya," Hannah whispers back.

Hannah is the only child of a teacher and a factory worker. Lonely, is the best way to describe an only child although some would say spoiled. Hannah is far from spoiled, since she must deal with strict parents about grades and curfew. Generally, Hannah is pretty good, but don't let all that quiet fool you. She can be quite rebellious.

Hannah calls once out in the car. "On my way out," she tells me. I live out in the country but not so far out that I wouldn't walk if need be. Once I walked to school in the dead of winter. It's not a far walk to school, but with the freezing cold, it was not one of my best ideas ever.

"I will wait in the garage for you," I reply. Not even going to say bye or leave a note this time. "What crap to have to wake up to every day?" I mutter to myself and the garage.

"Thanks, Hannah," I say as I close the car door.

"Sure anytime. We are headed over to Nicola's. I guess from there one of us can get Lena when the warden lets her out." Hannah laughs even though it's mean to say, it's true.

"Sounds good to me. Anything is better than being home right now," I say, probably sharing too much.

"What happened?" Hannah asks, but clearly not meaning to pry.

"Not one day can I wake up and not listen to my mom and Marie fight over something stupid. It's daily.

How can two people have that much to argue about? And of course, Lea can't just obey the rules and stay home. No, she must run off, so my parents have to drive all over the county looking for her. I just wish it would stop," I vent to Hannah more than I mean to, but it sure feels good to share the anguish with someone.

"Gosh, Rin, I am sorry. I didn't know it was like that for you every day. You always seem so happy."

"It's okay, Hannah. Thanks for listening. I just get frustrated and it felt good to let it out. Let's get to Nicola's and just enjoy the rest of the day."

Arriving at Nicola's, we see the rain hasn't stopped yet. In fact, it's gone from a downpour to a sprinkle. Hopefully, it'll stop before the whole day is ruined.

"Hi, girls. Nicola is downstairs checking on the pool," Tiffany says as she holds the door open. "Go ahead. I am sure you know the way." Tiffany is Nicola's stepmom and, in her twenties, and in Nicola's opinion, too young for her dad.

We make our way downstairs. "Nic, what's up with Tiffany?" I ask as I reach the bottom step.

"She has her undies in a wad because I invited you guys over to hang out which doesn't include her and Tyler," Nicola throws out.

"So, the usual," Hannah adds. Poor Tiffany. If Nicola even knew I was thinking that she would snap. Step-mommy is too close to our age and that is crazy. I couldn't imagine what Nicola must think, not good things I am sure.

"So obviously our plans have changed due to the rain. Cook is making up some sandwiches and snacks for us," Nicola informs us.

"Guess it's the pool today, huh?" Hannah asks.

"Yeah, but let's wait for Lena," Nicola says. "I brought my iPod down for some music. Who is going to call Lena?" Both Nicola and Hannah look at me.

"Really? Oh, all right." Somehow, I always seem to be the one who must call Lena's house. Not fun, I might add.

As the phone rings to Lena's, my mind starts to wander which of course causes a stumble over my tongue when Lena's mom picks up on the other end. Lena's mom isn't the nicest to Lena but when I call her mom, she puts on a huge façade even though we have all seen and heard her treat Lena like Cinderella.

"Um . . . is Lena there? This is Rin." I get it together enough to squeak out a plausible sentence.

"Well, hello, Rin. Yes, Lena is here somewhere. Let me get her." Lena's mom is acting somewhat normal. Wonder what is up.

"Hey, Rin," Lena says as she gets on the line.

"What's up?" Okay, so this is not Lena. The girl I am hearing is in too good of mood.

"Hey, Lena, so the rain has put a nice damper on our hike. We thought we all would hang out at Nicola's, enjoy the pool and whatever. Can you join us?" I look at Hannah and Nicola like I am talking to a stranger.

"Sure. Come on over and pick me up. I will be ready in ten." Lena hangs up before I can even spit out a reply.

Hanging up the phone, Hannah and Nicola are dying to know what just happened.

"Lena's mom was nice, and Lena was in a good mood. I could hear her smile," I tell them both. "It was weird."

"So, the warden is letting Lena out?" Nicola asks.

"Yeah. We can pick her up in ten." Nicola and Hannah look at each other then back at me.

"Are you kidding me? Neither of you will go pick her up?" As I extend my hand for the keys to Hannah's car, already knowing their response. "Wimps," I tell them as I roll my eyes at them both while heading for the stairs. "Be back soon – I hope."

"That was easy," Hannah says.

"Nah, we just lucked out by making Rin think we wouldn't go." They both laugh not realizing that I heard what they said.

****

Maybe Lena's mom was pleased that she managed to get all her chores done before work yesterday that today she is giving Lena some leniency, I think. Pulling up to Lena's, I start to see the real picture. Family's in from out of town, which is why everything is okay. Lena comes running to the car.

"Go!" she screams at me. Shocked by the change in her persona, I hit the gas and we are gone.

"What the heck?" Is all I can get out before Lena starts crying. I pull the car over so she can get this out before we get back to Nicola's.

"Thanks," Lena sobs out.

"What happened? You were so happy on the phone." Confused, I don't know what's going on.

"I had to clean the entire house this morning because family was coming to visit. Then I had to put on the act that 'life is great'. Oh, my mom can act very well," Lena explains still tearful. Now, it all makes sense.

"Wow," I manage to get out.

She sniffs and blows her nose in a tissue.

"Okay," she says, taking in a deep breath, "I am better. Thanks, Rin. Let's just pretend all is well and have a nice day." Lena, the one to pull herself together and make the best of things for the sake of others. I would have been mortified and probably still a complete mess even after we got back to Nicola's. Lena is strong though and tough, I must give her that.

"Did you remember your swimsuit?" I ask Lena before we get out of the car.

"You bet. I keep my bag packed and ready," she says as we both laugh heading downstairs to join antsy pants and Hannah.

"So, what happened?" they both ask us in unison.

"Oh, my mom has family visiting and didn't mind that I left," Lena shares, giving them a smoother version of what happened.

"Cool." Nicola and Hannah's big reply as they sit lounging on the lawn chairs.

"Well, we have sandwiches, chips with dip and soda." Nicola points to the bar inside the house where the cook has our snacks laid out for us.

"We pulled the pool cover off while you were gone. So, let's chat a bit and eat before hitting the water," Hannah says.

We all take and fill a plate. Hitting the couch, Nicola punches play on her iPod and music flows around us and out by the pool.

"So, Nicola." I turn to face her with my serious look.

"How was the dance the other night?" We all are dying for details even though we know that Treyton is his name and that he has liked Nicola forever.

"We all had a blast. Don't you remember, Rin, you were whining about how sore your feet were," Nicola spits back, knowing full well what I was really asking.

Lena and Hannah look at Nicola with smiles plastered across their faces knowing and thinking the same as me.

"What?" Is all Nicola can say as she heads to the pool dropping her shorts as she goes out the door

The three of us head to the changing rooms to put on our suits. We rush so we can get details that we know Nicola will spill.

"So, can you guys stay over?" Nicola asks us as soon as we are all wet and enjoying the water.

"I can," Hannah and I say together.

"Well, let me check with my mom," Lena says, dreading the phone call to her mom after the way the morning went before their company arrived.

"That works. Hannah can take us home to get clothes and such. While we are at my house you can ask your mom. We can pick you up last." I organize out the plan to give Lena enough time to pack clothes and do whatever chores the warden dishes out to her.

"Enough seriousness," Nicola hollers out as she cannonballs into the pool practically right on top of us.

Chapter Six

Ah, Saturday. I wake up at Nicola's thinking about not getting very far with the details on Nicola and Treyton yesterday, but we all know about the two of them.

"Rin, are you up?" Lena hollers across the hall. Oh, leave it to Lena to ruin a good thought. I laugh to myself.

"So, we didn't get to hike yesterday. Let's hit the East Bluff and Devils Doorway this morning before it gets too hot," Lena says.

"What else are we doing to do before work?" Nicola asks. "The lake is all that we do, and we love it."

"Let's go for some breakfast. I am sure cook has quite a spread ready for us." Nicola knows that we all love her cook like family.

Our shift begins at two-thirty today. So, of course we are all up early and as our drill sergeant commands, hitting the East Bluff. It's good to see her in better spirits than yesterday, I think, as I bound down the stairs to the kitchen.

We all love staying at Nicola's. It's like living on our own other than Tiffany and Tyler being around. We usually don't pay attention to them. Perhaps that's rude but we aren't over to entertain them.

"Let's get going," Lena commands as we all grab a freshwater bottle from the refrigerator and our backpacks ready with work clothes.

As usual, we park in the lot furthest away from the trailhead, walk past the South Shore store and find ourselves right in from of the trail map.

"We know the way, so I don't think we need to check the map again," Hannah complains. "Let's just get hiking."

I agree with Hannah. "We have hiked this so many times we know the way."

"Wait," Nicola says, "I have something for each of us to wear. I made these friendship bracelets from some old leather strands I found in the attic." The bracelets have an antique brown look to them, small, single strand of leather with a clasp to close on our wrists.

"These are great Nicola. I will wear mine every day and never take it off." I say, excited she thought of these and that each of us have one.

"Love it!" Hannah adds. "I will wear mine always."

"Ditto for me," Lena says as we all take turns helping each other put the bracelets on. "Onward!" Lena throws up a hand like charging into battle.

"Okay, let's do this!" Nicola yells out as we make our way down the trail through the canopy of trees above giving some shade that even makes it a bit cool this morning. The humidity hasn't risen, and the shade seems cooler.

Up Potholes Trail right through the puzzle piece and past the pothole bowls. Taking the trail to the left once at the top, we make our way down the trail to the steps that lead to Devils Doorway.

"Beautiful," I manage to say as we come up to the doorway. There is a light fog over the lake that gives it a beautiful view as well as eerie in a way.

Stepping through the doorway, suddenly, everything seems to change. Gone are the familiar shapes of trees as well as the park parking lot.

Now, all I see for miles are vineyards and several rows of cottages.

What on earth...?

There are people out in the yards playing some type of game and boats running on the lake. To our surprise, there are other hikers at the doorway and their clothing looked very different from ours.

"What just happened?" I ask as we take in this new and unfamiliar scenery. I glide back and forth through the doorway as if I missed something. But, no, when we step forward, we're wearing old clothes: ankle-length skirts, ruffles and buttoned-up ankle boots. When I step backward, I'm back in my shorts and T-shirt. Lena, Nicola and Hannah each take a turn walking back and forth through the doorway.

"Am I in a dream?" Lena asks, blinking fast. "Or is something *really* weird going on?"

"Excuse me," a small, polite voice interrupts Lena. "If you were dreaming, we would not see you or hear you."

Standing in awe, we all look at this small child who speaks well beyond her age. She can see us.

"She is right," Hannah says in almost a whisper. Turning to the small girl, she asks, "Where are we?" Hannah bends down at the girl's level with knees touching the cool rock.

"Devils Lake," the girl answers all giggly, watching us appear and disappear.

"But . . . how can this be?" Nicola asks in a calm voice stepping back through the doorway watching her clothes change. Lena walks over and collectively, with all her cool, asks the little girl, "What year is it?"

"The year is 1891," the little girl answers in awe of the magic she is seeing. The four of us just stand there. We are all speechless. How did we get here? This must be a mistake.

Even Lena is quiet, which is unusual for her. She usually has an explanation, idea or plan for all situations. But not this one.

"We need to go back through the doorway. We can't stay here," Lena says almost frantic.

"I agree with Lena," Hannah replies. "What if we can't go back?" Our fellow hikers are kindly standing by, perhaps to answer more of our questions.

Why do they not ask some of their own? I wonder to myself. Has this happened before? They do not seem surprised and are relaxed about this.

"The music is starting early, Momma. Can we go?" The little girl asks. The distant sound of music flows up the bluff in our direction. It has a good beat.

"We are going to the pavilion. You are welcome to join us," the small polite girl tells us. "Just follow the music."

Our new friends leave us.

Hannah takes a step through the doorway to go back but remains in her ankle-length skirt and buttoned-up ankle boots.

"Guys, I think we are stuck here." Hannah tries again to go back to our time and to no avail is still with us.

"Lena, you try. You were the first one through the doorway," I say nervously, biting my nails and wondering how we will get home now. Lena tries and she is still dressed as we are. No more T-shirt and shorts.

"Guess we are stuck for now. May as well make the best of it and see what the lake looks like in 1891," Lena says, not convincing us that she is okay or that we really will get home again.

"Let's go." Nicola stands up anxiously. "We all love music and they seem quite nice." Lena scowls at Nicola.

"Don't you understand? How are we going to get home? How did we get here? 1891, really?"

"Come on, Lena. What could it hurt? This is a once in a lifetime experience. No one back home will believe us." I try to keep everyone calm.

"I am with Rin on this one," Hannah pipes in. "We have never seen the lake this way before. Perhaps, we could learn something from this era."

"Come on, Lena," the three of us say.

"Oh, all right." Lena cracks a smile. "What could it hurt? Besides, we all look very hip in these dresses." We all laugh and head back through the doorway to follow the music.

"Are you kidding me?" All four of us say together, as we are now back in 2018. We look down and see we're wearing the same shorts and shirts from before.

"We had to have dreamt, that right?" Lena asks, almost afraid.

"No, Lena, we were all there," I tell her, as Nicola and Hannah nod their heads in agreement with me.

"Let's head back down to the beach and enjoy our afternoon cooling off," Nicola says matter-of-factly.

Lena is unusually quiet as we hike Potholes Trail back down. Going down is way easier than up. We still must be careful though, as the rocks that make the path are even more slippery going down.

Lena, Nicola, Hannah or I have not said a word since we started our decent down the bluff, along the scree path, back across the railroad tracks and right past the store and canoes.

Walking right past the South Shore store, I wonder where the pavilion is and try picturing where the vineyards and orchards are.

Reaching our beach, as we call it, we unpack towels, and sunscreen all the while not one of us says a word.

"Did we really go back in time?" Nicola whispers quietly as we lay out our beach towels.

"Yes, we did. We were all there," I say, loud enough to make the point and try to stop the curious thoughts running through everyone's heads.

"I just don't understand that when we passed through the doorway checking. Why couldn't we see then and now? Why didn't the people we saw there ask any questions of their own?" Lena finally says, trying to rationalize what happened.

"Listen, we can sit here trying to . . . I don't know, figure it out or hit the water and cool off this sweat before we have to get ready for work," Hannah chimes in. She just wants to swim.

"For once, Hannah makes a good point!"

"Rin, you don't have to be so loud," Lena strikes back.

"Now that's the Lena we all know," I say. Hannah and Nicola nod in agreement, as we take off racing toward the water.

Chapter Seven

Beep! Beep! Goes the horn on Hannah's car as she sits out front of my house.

"Let's go!" Nicola says. "Off to pick up Lena."

"I sure hope Lena's mom doesn't give her a hard time like usual," Hannah says.

"Oh, you know she will," Nicola adds.

"Well, this should be fun," I toss out, knowing exactly what this will be like as I crawl into the back seat of Hannah's car.

Pulling up to Lena's, we all get out of the car. No sense in waiting outside because we all know what awaits. Either Lena is having a big fight with her mom or complete silence.

All three of us walk through the door. The silence is deafening. "Lena!" Hannah hollers out.

"Thanks a lot, Hannah. You just scared the crap out of me," I yell at her.

"Upstairs," Lena yells down to us.

"Hey, are you ready?" I ask as the three of us reach the top step seeing Lena buried in baskets of laundry.

"Um, no. I have a long list of chores to do before work or I will be at this all night after work." Lena shows us her list that her mom left her.

- Unload and reload dishwasher, run

- Hand wash what doesn't fit in dishwasher

- Finish the laundry and put away

- Make supper for sisters

"Let's all help," I chime in.

"Yeah," Hannah and Nicola say together.

"Where are your sisters?" I ask, knowing that if we help Lena and they know, they will tattle.

"They went down to the swimming pool," Lena says. "About fifteen minutes ago."

"Okay, so its two o'clock now and we don't have to be to work until five and the pool closes at four thirty. That gives us until at least four fifteen to conquer this long list," I say matter-of-factly.

Of course, leave it to Lena's mom to put this all on her. I think to myself while I head back downstairs to the kitchen. We each take a chore and get started. We also decided to each chip in for food for all of us including Lena's sisters.

"Thank you, Rin," Lena says meekly.

"You're welcome. We are all here for each other. It's what friends do."

Lena may sound like a drill sergeant at times, but I believe it's because of the treatment she gets at home from her mom. Makes her feel somewhat in control of something in her life.

Nicola, Hannah and I know this, but we still love to make fun of her, and Lena knows we are just kidding and that we know her home life is comparable to Cinderella without the Fairy Godmother and Prince to make it all better. In due time, I suppose.

What are friends for? So, Hannah, Nicola and I will leave to pick up supper and come back as if we were never there to help Lena. This way her sisters can't tell on her for getting some help with chores.

Lena's sisters are like that. They like to see Lena get into trouble and have more chores dumped on her. The whole "watch your sisters" is crap too. They are both old enough to watch themselves and have before.

"Okay, let's go pick up some food," I tell Hannah and Nicola.

"Lena, just finish up what you are working on and act like you really didn't seem to mind all the chores," I say as the three of us head out to our local A&W that still provides car side ordering.

****

"We brought supper," I say, holding up the bag as if I'd just gotten there. "We even got paper plates and such for a quick clean up. We don't want to be late for work." I set the bags on the table and hand out plates and food.

82

"Let's eat!" Miss antsy pants Nicola says eagerly. We all laugh, even Lena's sisters. They don't have a clue as to what had gone on while they were swimming, but we will always know.

Chapter Eight

We work our way into Wednesday again.
Arriving at the lake, it is in full swing for this
sweltering, hot humid summer day. All four of us are
grateful to have access to air conditioning throughout
our shift. Huge fans run in the Chateau along the dance
floor. We all keep busy in our perspective jobs longing
for our shift to end so we can relax for the dance.

"Let's wrap it up," I tell Kip so we can get over to
the chateau and help close out the night before the dance
starts. "How is everyone doing?" I ask as Kip and I
waltz through the doors of the chateau after closing the
snack shop.

"I finished the gift shop," Hannah says, carrying
her deposit to the safe.

"Nate and I are just about done over here," Lena hollers across the dance floor where the two of them are finishing up the sweeping.

****

Same old, same old DJ every week so the music stays pretty much the same. Nicola and Treyton are off dancing while Lena, Hannah and I stand along the wall as if it were going to fall over.

"Ha, I never thought any one of us would have a summer boyfriend," Hannah snorts out in a laugh.

"I am glad Nicola does. She seems happy," Lena shares, getting a little emotional.

I just stand and watch, thinking that Nicola and Treyton are more than a summer fling.

"I am glad we are all staying the night at Nicola's. Let's hike the East Bluff again to Devils Doorway." I want to try one more time. See if somehow, the magic is still there.

"Sounds good to me," Lena answers, which isn't a surprise to any of us since we figure she is probably devising a plan on how to torture us. I laugh to myself at this thought.

"What are you smiling about?" Lena demands to know.

I point to Treyton and Nicola on the dance floor, as he dips her during their dance hoping to divert the attention from me.

Nicola comes running over. "I am having a blast," she says excitedly while grabbing our arms and dragging us to the dance floor. Good thing the DJ plays excellent music, which keeps everyone moving and the dance floor full.

****

What a great night's sleep. I don't think I have slept this good in quite a long time. I am lost in my thoughts and for a change, not allowing Lena's constant nagging from down the hall get to me.

Slam! The door hits the wall as Lena bursts through it.

"Really? Lena you could have put a hole in that wall!" I yell at her even though the slam of the door should have scared me or at least caught me off guard, but it doesn't. Guess being raised to know how to open a door is what took over my instincts.

"Sorry, miss grouchy pants. Didn't you hear me calling you for breakfast?" Lena asks not even feeling a bit bad for opening the door that way.

"I am not grouchy."

As I bound down the stairs without much care, the next thing I know I am going head over heels as I fall to the bottom. Before I even realize what happened, everyone from the kitchen is around me asking if I am okay.

"Oh my gosh, are you hurt?"

"You all right? I was right behind you and couldn't believe what I was seeing," Lena says in disbelief.

"I am fine. I think I may have a bruise on my hip. What the heck happened? Did I trip? Slip? What?" I am usually stable on my feet, so this is beyond words.

"Oh, I am sorry, Rin," Tiffany says from the stairs as the four of us turn to look at her.

"What for?"

"One of Tyler's toys was on that step there," she says, pointing to the step.

"He just recently started climbing the stairs and I guess I didn't realize he was carrying toys as well."

"It's okay, Tiffany. I am fine, a little bruised, but, truly, I am fine." I try to reassure her as Nicola stares at Tiffany with a crinkled-up nose and squinting eyes that you must wonder if her eyes are still open.

Lena reaches over and helps me off the floor while Hannah gives Nicola a good smack on the back of the head Dinozzo/Gibbs style.

"Ah, family love," I blurt out and laugh, trying to keep the air light and not so serious. "Let's get some breakfast!" I yell out as I head off to the kitchen to see what divine dish Nicola's cook tossed together for us.

"So, East Bluff again, huh, Rin?" Lena raises her eyebrows at me like I am crazy.

"Yes. I am hoping we run into our new friends and perhaps get to spend more time with them in their era," I whisper so only the four of us can hear.

"That is all I can think of, too. Do you really think, we will see them again?" Lena questions me like a little kid in a candy store.

"Do you really think it is safe for us to even try again?" Hannah asks the question we are all really thinking in the back of our minds wanting to not worry about it.

"Why wouldn't it be safe?" Nicola answers, not really understanding Hannah's concern.

"Well, we were there back in time crossing back and forth through the doorway and couldn't really see the then and now. What happens if we cross over again and can't get back?" Hannah makes a good point.

"Didn't think of it like that. I guess I was thinking that we may be unsafe in an unknown place and era. I never considered we could get stuck there," I reply.

"Goodness, I didn't even think of it like that either," Lena says.

"Should we still go then?" Hannah asks.

"Yes, I think we should. We won't get stuck there. I am sure of it," I answer not positive we wouldn't get stuck there but really, how could we.

"Yes, I agree with Rin," Lena says which is unlike her to want to take a chance. Nicola hasn't really said much as to whether we should or not. She seems to just follow whatever we do.

"Let's head out then," Hannah says, humming to "Banana Pancakes" by Jack Johnson as she trots out the front door. We all laugh and follow her eloquent exit humming the same tune.

As usual, we arrive early in the morning before the humidity and all the campers are moving about on the trails. The smell penetrating from the campfires takes me back to memories of camping when I was small.

"That's what we should do!" Hannah gets excited.

"What are you jumping about?" Lena demands to know. Nicola is laughing and I am tagging along behind as we make our usual walk past the canoes, store and beach.

"We should all go camping," Hannah explains in her own matter-of-fact way.

"I am down with that," Nicola adds, still humming "Banana Pancakes," that Hannah had started earlier.

"Gosh, I haven't been camping in forever. I wonder if my parent's tent is still in good shape." I remember back briefly of having our tent pitched in the back yard and my neighbor friend and I camping out. We made ourselves quite freaked out one time.

"A tent? Who needs that? It's way too hot for a tent. I say we just rent a site and camp out under the stars," Lena shares with us.

"At least there are no mosquitoes out."

"Yeah, too humid even for them to be biting and dying." We all laugh as Nicola tells her rendition of the life span of a mosquito.

"So, are we stopping at the trail map this time, Lena?" I ask sarcastically knowing that we didn't bother to last time we hiked.

"No, I am thinking that since we didn't do things exactly as we usually do is how our friends appeared," Lena explains, perhaps a little superstitious but we all nod our heads in agreement even if we don't believe it completely.

It's not like Lena to think that way. She is usually more logical. I am going to guess that our friends from another time have her all frazzled.

Chapter Nine

Reaching the beginning of Potholes Trail, we start up the path single file.

"I swear, this path was purposely made this way, so no one can breathe," Hannah puffs out.

"I . . . know. I think my . . . heart is going to pound right out of my chest," Nicola manages to say while gasping.

"Let's take a break here," I suggest as we are just below that puzzle piece of rock, my favorite mystery on any trail.

"A break is good. We have managed to hike this far without taking one." Hannah and Nicola follow suit as we each take a seat on a cool rock. We sit catching our breath just looking around at the view from our perch.

Finally reaching the top, we take our usual left on to the East Bluff Trail to head down to Devils Doorway. Arriving at the doorway, we all stand in awe at the beauty before us as the lake comes to life with early morning hikers and those getting ready to venture out on their kayaks.

"Gosh, this is just too serene," I manage a whisper. It's beautiful, yes, but part of me thinks about the past. How different did the view look in 1891?

"My thoughts exactly!" Nicola shares quietly while Hannah nods her head in agreement and for a nice change Lena is quiet allowing us all to enjoy the low haze of humidity that is arriving and the green roll of the bluffs as they surround the lake while the birds and other nature animals scurry about their day.

One by one, we each find our own place to perch for a bit. We can hear the kayakers making conversation almost as if we were right there with them. The lake allows a voice to carry easily up the bluffs.

Lena stands as we all look at her, and we know she wants to go through the doorway. Perhaps today we can pass through another time, see the lake in a different but almost same manner.

Not one of us is talking as we help each other up into the doorway. We each stand there looking at the view, all thinking the same things. Will we end up right here or be in 1891 once we walk through the doorway.

"Well, I guess this is it," Lena says as we all are eager to go.

"Let's do this!" Nicola hollers out.

"Thanks Nicola. You just scared the crap out of us." We are all nervous wrecks, as our hopes are high.

"Okay, let's go. We keep standing here as if this will happen without us moving a muscle," Hannah says quietly. We all wait for one of us to make the first move. You would think we were scared. The last time we just walked through without much thought, but the view was different.

"All right, I am going through." I start to move through the doorway and Lena, Nicola, and Hannah follow suit.

As we begin walking through, our T-shirts, shorts and tennis shoes are replaced with tight sleeves to our arms, capped at the shoulders with ruffles, fitted to our wrists. The skirt fits more closely over our hips with a flare just above the knee and the skirt length is inches from the earth and with tall lace-up shoes. Our long hair drapes about our shoulders, longing to be tied up from the humidity.

I wonder to myself how they handle this humidity with all these clothes on and at the same time, I am happy to be in this time again.

Not one of us is saying a word. Perhaps we are hoping this time we can stay for a bit.

"Well, good day, ladies," a gentleman kindly says to us.

"Good day," I return the gesture with a small smile and nod of my head. I wonder how they just seem to accept us as if we have been here all along.

"Won't you join us for our picnic?" he politely asks.

"Thank you," I answer back while Lena, Nicola and Hannah stand speechless, watching my interaction with this man.

The man and his family make room for the four of us while we climb back down from the doorway. Not an easy task I might add in long dresses that we are not used to wearing.

"Look," Lena says pointing down toward the south end of the lake. Each of us takes in this beautiful view of the lake. Along the shoreline, there is a line of small cottages and just behind them sit two larger buildings. Behind each of those buildings, the trees are replaced with vineyards, orchards and what looks like farmland. A roadway runs east and west between the properties.

"Wow," Nicola and Hannah say quietly.

"It's just gorgeous," I manage in a whisper.

"Come, join us," the man's small-voiced wife eagerly says as she pats the picnic blanket with her tiny hand.

Her husband adorns a gray coat with covered buttons and matching waistcoat, dark trousers, short turnover shirt collar and a floppy bow tie. His hair is kept short and is a dark brown almost black in color matching his soft mustache and pointed beard.

"Let's sit and not keep them waiting. We don't want to seem rude and impolite," I tell Nicola, Lena and Hannah as none of them seem to have found their tongues.

"Thank you, ma'am."

"Oh, please call me Elizabeth and my husband is Arthur. Those young boys there are James and Oscar."

Elizabeth points to the east where her two boys are frolicking from one rock to another.

Elizabeth adorns the same type of shirt, skirt and shoes that we are dressed in. Only difference is her hair is done very nicely up off her neck in a tight bun.

"Thank you, Elizabeth. My name is Rin and my friends are Lena, Nicola and Hannah."

"So, ladies, where do you hail from?" Arthur asks hoping that he may know their parents.

"We're from Gem City." I know that they are wondering why they haven't met us before. I managed to get some research on Gem City which is what our hometown was called back in the 1890's. Easier to make conversation with them if I can refer to it by the name they know.

"Come now. Lunch is ready," Elizabeth interrupts my thoughts. Spread out before us is mouth-watering fried chicken, corn bread, apple salad, chocolate cake and sweet iced tea.

"Wow, what a spread," Nicola says excited to be enjoying such a delicious meal.

"We usually have a meat sandwich or sub sandwich with chips and water," Hannah chimes in not realizing that Arthur and Elizabeth may not have a clue to what a sub sandwich might be.

Everyone calms down and enjoys the fine lunch spread before us. Small chit-chat about the weather and simple things make the time fly.

"Thank you very much for sharing your lunch with us." Lena and I stand and walk to the edge to take in this new view while Nicola and Hannah help Elizabeth pack up the picnic basket.

"Tell us more about the lake as we view it right now. Could we have a tour and see what there is to do here?" Lena asks, saving the day. Technically, we are from another time, but we can't ruin their hopes and dreams of how they see the lake.

"Sure. Elizabeth, are we ready to head back down?" Arthur asks his wife without much thought to our deterring his question.

"Yes, Arthur. We are ready." Elizabeth gathers her boys and the blanket while Arthur collects the picnic basket from our picnic spot.

"After you ladies," Arthur says as he points the way up the stairs. We all stop at the top with Elizabeth and wait for Arthur, Oscar and James. Arthur takes the lead down the trail to the left, "ladies are you coming?"

"Go ahead, we will catch up," I answer Arthur while Lena, Hannah and Nicola stop and back up to where I am standing.

"What now?" Lena asks gruffly.

"If we leave the trail and go down to the lake, do you think we will make it back through the doorway?" I ask the question we are all thinking.

"I didn't think of that. Last time we were here we didn't leave the doorway," Lena says.

"Exactly! So, if we leave the trail, we have to think again of the chance of us getting stuck here," Hannah states wanting to ensure we won't be stuck in 1891 indefinitely.

"I agree." Nicola finally puts in some decision one way or another. "We do not know if we will get back through once we leave the doorway."

"We have already left the doorway and are standing here on the trail headed toward Balanced Rock. Do we want to just stay here at the doorway and never see the lake in this era up close?" Lena makes a good point about being away from the doorway, but I am still not sure we should really leave any further than we already have.

"Let's just do it," Hannah says because she is sick of the arguing even though she is worried too that we could get stuck in this time.

"Ladies, is everything alright?" Arthur asks. We didn't notice that he had come back down near Devil's Doorway to see where we were.

"Yes, everything is good," I answer as I wonder how much of our conversation he overheard. "Let's go guys." The four of us leave the doorway and venture down the trail with Arthur to Balanced Rock Trail.

Chapter Ten

Arthur chooses Balanced Rock Trail down. The stairs are made from wood just like a regular staircase in a home would be. There is a handrail made from tree branches, smooth to the touch. The trail leads almost along the same as our trail but is safer. No slippery rocks and there is a handrail.

"Be careful now. These stairs can be tricky," Arthur warns us as we make our way down and right past Balanced Rock. As we reach the bottom, Arthur lends a hand for each of us to take as we descend the last step, very much a gentleman.

"That was quite a trip," Hannah says as Lena, Nicola and my-self all nod in agreement. We are all thinking about the hike back up in these dresses and shoes. How do they do it? Taking the trail that runs parallel to the railroad tracks, we come to the same fork in the trail much like in our time.

This time to our left there is a small white one level home surrounded by trees and a nice yard. The windows are long and narrow. The front porch dons a gable roof with wood shingles and decorative columns. Hanging from the porch roof is a sign that reads "Kirkland." Along the right side of the house is another smaller porch with an old-fashioned milk can sitting next to the door.

"Look." Hannah points toward the small house. We all stand in awe of its character. How the home seems to fit perfectly along the East Bluff. It is a different view for us as we are used to dense woods.

"Ladies, we have to cross the railroad tracks, just this way." Arthur points to the right and the path looks familiar except for the bridge.

This is great. We get firsthand views of what the lake looked like long before our own time. I feel as though I am dreaming.

Taking the path to the right we head toward the railroad tracks. We stop to watch as the cattle make their way home as we cross the bridge to the railroad tracks and over to the other side. Their trail follows along the tracks. Reaching the railroad tracks, we stop. Here in this time there are two sets.

"Check it out," Hannah says gesturing to our left down the tracks, where there sit three buildings.

"Let's check them out," I say without much thought and start walking down the tracks. Hannah,

Nicola and Lena follow suit and before long, we are standing in front of the train depot with a ticket office and two platforms on either side of the tracks. In our time, this is where the South Shore Road crosses the tracks going toward the CCC camp.

Making our way back down the railroad tracks back to where we stepped off the bridge, we cross over to where Arthur and his family wait for us.

"Ladies, are you set for your tour?" Arthur asks us.

"Arthur, whose house is that?" Lena asks pointing back across the railroad tracks to the house that sits along the East Bluff.

"That house, ladies, belongs to the Kirk family. I will introduce you to them," Arthur shares as we follow him to the stairs down from the platform. We chatter amongst ourselves as we follow Arthur and his family down the path.

"Look at that!" Nicola hollers out excitedly pointing at the large building in front of us.

"That is the Kirkland Hotel," Arthur explains before we can ask. The Kirkland Hotel is two stories and appears to be placed just by the left of the bird wing facing the lake. "So, the bird mound has been here for quite some time," Lena acknowledges quietly and only so we can hear.

"Arthur, can we have a look around the inside?" I ask, eager to see this historic building in every aspect.

"Of course!" Arthur excitedly answers back.

"If you will excuse us," Elizabeth says, "James, Oscar and myself have chores to attend to. Join us later this afternoon for drinks on the shore." We watch as they walk along the path toward the south end of the lake.

"Come." Arthur motions forward with his hand toward the hotel. I have time to give tours."

"Thank you. We are very appreciative." From somewhere, our politeness has emerged, and I wonder where it has been. As we walk along the north side of the Kirkland, Arthur points out the bird effigy showing that the hotel sits a portion atop of the bird's tail.

Coming around to the front of the Kirkland, we can see the lake. The calm of the water shows a glass like reflection of the beautiful bluffs.

"I have lost count of the cottages," Hannah says in awe as she stares at the shoreline.

"Yes, there are many," Arthur shares, "each with three rooms, screen porch facing the lake, own swimming beach and a dock with a rowboat."

"Now that would be perfect," Nicola says recalling our plans to rent a campsite.

"Sleeping along the lake, listening to all that peace." I can't think of better place.

Turning to face the front of the Kirkland, we all stand in awe at its beauty. Stepping up onto the big open porch, we turn and face the lake.

"A whole new view of the lake," Hannah points out.

"Right this way, ladies." Arthur opens the door to the Kirkland and we all step through the doorway slowly.

Straight in front is a small lobby. Along the back wall, a desk stands for check-in and to the left of the desk is the post office. To the immediate right of the desk is a large beautiful staircase making its way to the second level.

As we turned to the right, we see a large dining room with guests and public welcome for any meal. Back through the lobby, there is a lounge with a large fireplace and seating for anyone who wants to relax and chat.

The back of the hotel holds the kitchen and a small office. All meals for the Kirkland are prepared right in that kitchen with ingredients from locals. The upper level holds fourteen sleeping rooms.

"This is just beautiful," I say quietly.

"Not too bad for an old rustic place," Arthur says.

"Yes, it is rustic but quite beautiful," Lena adds as if copying me. We all stand in the lounge in awe as we have never seen such a gorgeous, natural fireplace. In our time, most are run on gas not wood and they are not built this large.

Stepping back out on to the big porch, we stop and view the lake again. Many cottages line up along the shore and I cannot wait to check them out.

"Let's head down this path here." Arthur ushers us to the right. "We will view the cottage here on the end nearest the cattle watering hole. If you rent this cottage, you get the best fishing area on this side of the lake."

"This is great. Thank you, Arthur, for taking time to show us around," Nicola says.

"You are quite welcome," he replies. "I need to check on Elizabeth and my boys; you ladies feel free to wander about. Anyone here will be happy to answer any questions you may have." Arthur leaves us at the cottage and makes his way south across the lake.

"Just look, there is another large building past the Kirkland." Hannah points down the path.

"It would be great to spend an entire day here," Lena says. "I say we rent our campsite and do just that."

"Yes, let's do that," Nicola agrees with Lena.

"We need to find out what time it is," I say. "I think our time here today is running low and if we are going to get back up to the doorway, we need to get going so it won't be dark." I get all technical and try not to pull the work card, but it is evident that we must go.

"Let's go back to the Kirkland Hotel and see if there is a clock," Hannah suggests. "If I remember correctly there was a clock on the fireplace." We re-enter the Kirkland and find the fireplace and sure

enough there is a clock on the mantel.

"It's time to head back home or we will be late for

work," I say as we make our way back outside.

Chapter Eleven

Making our way back toward Balanced Rock Trail, we are all wondering if there is a trail up Potholes just like this one.

"This will be a challenge," Hannah states matter-of-factly. We all laugh as we know she is right.

"At least there are actual stairs with a handrail," Lena adds while trying to keep a straight face. We stand at the bottom of the stairway, waiting for other hikers to descend before we can start up.

"I just can't believe how different everything looks. It's like a dream to be here and experience this firsthand," Nicola says quietly.

Arriving back at the doorway, each of us takes a few minutes to enjoy the view of the lake as it is in 1891.

"Well, I am guessing that we should wait for hikers to leave before we try to go back through the doorway," Lena whispers to me quietly.

"I agree, but I think we can make an effort to climb up there, so we are ready," I say.

We don't rush, making our way to the doorway, as we try to decide the best way to climb up with all these clothes on.

"Let's hoist Rin up first. She is smaller and a little bit lighter," Lena suggests so we don't all look silly trying to make our way up.

"Sounds good, Lena." I nod in agreement.

Taking our time, we each make the climb up into the doorway. Standing patiently, enjoying the view, we wait for the remainder of the hikers to move on down the path so we can cross back through to our time.

"I am going to miss this. It is like we have been on a mini vacation," Hannah shares, sounding a bit sad.

"I very much agree," Lena adds.

"Oh, guys, we can come back. This is the second time we have been here, and I think we will be back again," Nicola excitedly shares jumping up and down like a kid in a candy store. We all laugh at this as we all know she is right.

"We will get to visit again and see more," I share as each one of us takes our place and walks back through the doorway. Once again, we are home.

We make it back down to Hannah's car and we rush off to the North Shore for work. As usual, the lake is booming with many visitors trying to get reprieve from the heat and humidity.

I catch up with Kip at the Snack Shop. It feels like forever since we have worked but it's only been a day.

"How's it going, Kip?" I ask, knowing that his answer will be the same as it usually is.

"You know it." There it is. A simple reply, not that it really tells me how he is doing but I have come to expect the usual laid-back answers Kip has. It is probably due to his carefree attitude, which seems to make this job perfect for him.

****

"Hey, Rin, how's it going?" Lena asks with a brief stop at the Snack Shop.

"It's great. Busy, but that makes time fly by." Wow, she looks happy for a change.

"Yes, busy is good. I must get back. Hannah is helping Nicola and Nate's alone in there," she says, gesturing toward the Chateau.

Kip returns from his break and I nod at him.

"Okay, Kip, I am going to take a short break. I already took care of some of the clean-up but if you want to start with the Icee machines that would be great."

I head out for a brisk walk. I have no doubt that Kip will get that stuff done so when I get back, we can count the cash drawer and head over to the Chateau.

Kip and I walk through the door expecting to help finish up the clean-up in the Chateau. Standing there, I can't believe what I am seeing. Nate and Lena chatting away and sweeping together? I must have missed the memo where she decided to be nice to Nate. Guess that gives me something to tease her about. I chuckle to myself.

"Are you two all caught up?" I ask as if I didn't see anything.

"Yes, we are Rin," Lena answers for them both.

"What a great afternoon. I may have to spend more time in rentals. Way more to see there," Hannah shares as she and Nicola make their way out to the floor where the rest of us are standing.

We all leave work with large smiles on our faces. It had been a great day at the lake and work was just as good.

"So, guys, I got invited to a campsite after work and I am supposed to bring some friends. Anyone up for a campfire and hanging out?" Nicola asks us with an excited and begging look on her face.

"I am in," Hannah replies all giggly. "Rin? Lena?" They both look at us with faces your own grandmother couldn't say no to.

"I don't know. I think I would rather hang out and talk about the doorway and when we can go back," I say eager to get back to 1891.

"Oh, I like that idea better," Hannah says as we finish closing the chateau for the night and head down to the beach.

Chapter Twelve

"Hey Rin, what's up?" Hannah whispers. I am used to this with Hannah because her dad sleeps during the day.

"What do you have planned for today?" I ask quietly.

"I was just sitting thinking about our hike the other day," Hannah whispers. "Hold on a second, Rin. I am going to go sit out on the back porch so we can chat." I listen as Hannah attempts to walk quietly through the house to the back door.

"That's better," Hannah finally says into the phone. "I'm sitting on the porch.

"What did you have in mind?"

"How about you and I go out to the lake, sit and enjoy. Maybe walk along the lower trail on the West Bluff and just sit," I say trying to keep the peacefulness about the morning that she, too, was enjoying.

"Sounds great. I will get my stuff and pick you up in fifteen."

"Great. I will throw some snacks together and be ready." My mind is spinning with all kinds of snacks I could grab but a couple packs of Chex mix should suffice for this morning.

Glad Hannah was up to this, I think to myself, knowing it must be hard to be an only child and practically living in a commune where quiet is preferred. I have siblings and you would think life is great but just like everyone else, no one really knows what goes on behind closed doors.

"Hey, Hannah," I say, jumping in the car grateful to be out of the house.

"Let's park on the North Shore, easier to get to the trail." Hannah smiles for once feeling in control of a hike for a change.

"Look at that." She points at the lake as the fog lingers just inches above the water showing only the hints of rock that sit along the shore. Hannah stares in awe of its peaceful look.

Getting out of the car, we stand quietly, listening for sounds of life. Birds chirp and squirrels scurry up the trees. No human life can be heard, although it is early.

"Almost too quiet here. Kind of eerie." Hannah quietly walks over by me, eyebrows raised.

"Relaxing and peaceful is what this view says to me," I whisper back with a smirk on my face which makes her laugh. "Let's walk."

We walk across the grass this time rather than taking the path down to the Chateau and in front of the beach. We stop and view the effigy markers and finally reach the trail.

"The closer to the bluff and the water, the more difficult it is to see," Hannah says, not bothering to whisper, and her voice is loud in the silence. Her facial expression shows how serious she is which makes me laugh. Laughing together, we link arms and down the trail we go. We don't talk much, which is okay, as we enjoy the beauty of the lake as the fog slowly starts to lift from the water.

Turning to face the water, I add, "Look there, we are not the only ones enjoying the quiet here." We wave to the kayakers making their way along the shoreline.

"So, what were you thinking of our hike?" I look at Hannah with wide eyes anticipating her response.

"It seemed almost magical. So peaceful and calm." My thoughts exactly. "What about you?"

"Hannah, I can't wait to go back. There was so much to see and do there. I felt like I was on vacation." I laugh.

"Me either. I can't help wondering why Arthur and his family seem to take to us so easily. I mean wouldn't they wonder how we had just appeared," Hannah says.

"Yes, I was wondering the same thing. Let's talk more about this with Lena and Nicola later." I suggest still wondering that very thing.

"Thanks for calling me this morning. I really didn't know what I was going to do all day. Sitting at home in the quiet is too much," Hannah says with a deep look on her face.

"Hannah, I was glad you were free. We can both enjoy this. I would have come out alone if you had other plans."

"Oh, Rin, I never have any plans other than work and our hikes. So, we can enjoy together either in silence or small talk," Hannah answers back excitedly and grateful to be out of the house.

"Let's sit here." I leap to a nice big flat rock that sits closest to the water.

"Cold, rock is cold." Hannah carefully places her bare legs down on the rock.

"So, what do you make of Lena and Nate?" I ask curiously hoping I am not the only one who has noticed the two of them last night at work.

"What about them?" Hannah asks without a clue.

"Last night, Kip and I finished up early and just as we are walking into the Chateau, I notice Nate and Lena standing together, each holding a broom and laughing." I filled her in on what happened. "I then walked in, acting like I didn't see anything."

"You're kidding me?" Hannah asks in disbelief. "Lena, laughing?"

"I swear, she looked like she was enjoying herself," I say, surprised that Hannah didn't notice, unless it all started after she went out to help Nicola.

"Did you ask her about it?" Hannah wants to know.

"I haven't talked to her since you dropped me off last night."

"Oh, this is going to be fun. I can't wait to get the scoop on this one." Hannah smiles, evil like. We both laugh because we know that Lena will deny it all.

Chapter Thirteen

"Lena!" I holler after Lena and Nicola from the rock Hannah and I are lounging on.

"Oh, my gosh! We were just talking about you two," Lena hollers back as she and Nicola turn around to walk to where Hannah and I are.

"What are you two up to?" I ask as Lena and Nicola hop from rock to rock.

"Well, the day started out like crap, which is normal, but then we decided to come out here for a nice walk. How about you two?" Lena asks wondering how they all seemed to have the same idea.

"Pretty much the same as you guys," Hannah replies. "Too gorgeous of a day for sitting at home."

"No wonder people think we have no life. Here we are spending every day we can at the lake *and* work here," Nicola says with a serious straight-faced look. We all bust out laughing. Not from what she said, but just her seriousness.

"Where did you two park? We didn't see Hannah's car on the south end," Lena demands to know.

"Ma'am, we parked at the north end in the employee lot," I answer, saluting Lena sitting with my back nice and straight waiting for her to return the salute. The longer I sit like that, the more I can't seem to keep from laughing. We all laugh so hard we almost fall off the rock into the water.

"Whoa! Hold on," Hannah says, grabbing my arm. Lena doesn't find this too funny at first, decides it would be more fun to help me fall in.

Drenched, I work my way back to the rock as Hannah tries to help me up. Instead, I just pull her in with me. Nicola doesn't wait for someone to push or pull her in, she just jumps in on her own. Lena follows suit as we all splash about, enjoying the water.

"Guess swimsuits are overrated today," Lena hollers.

"Sure, beats skinny dipping," Nicola gurgles out with the water she is spitting from her mouth.

Reaching the rock after our short cooling off, we each hoist ourselves up onto it. "That was great," Hannah says laying on her back.

"I agree." Nicola sits down next to Hannah.

"So, Lena, how are things with you and Nate?" Hannah asks as I turn and glare at her with evil eyes. I wasn't ready to let Lena know any of us had a clue.

Gritting my teeth, I hold back the want to smack Hannah upside the head DiNozzo style.

"What is that supposed to mean?" Lena snottily asks.

"Well, you just seemed relaxed and . . . nice to him at work last night," Hannah guesses and an easy way to try to cover up from opening her big mouth. *Nice save, Hannah.*

"Is it a crime for me to be nice once in a while?" Lena snaps, annoyed.

"I guess not. Sorry I asked," Hannah says with a smirk on her face.

"Well, let's finish our walk and then go for lunch." Nicola changes the subject to ease the tension.

"Good idea. Since you two were walking toward the North end, here are my keys and bring my car over by Nicola's. We can decide from there where to have lunch," Hannah says as she rings water out of her hair.

"Sounds good," Nicola answers with her hand out for Hannah's keys.

We all meet at the South Shore where Nicola parked. "Where do we want to go for lunch?" I ask so we get that decided.

"Let's just hit a pizza joint," Nicola says, jumping up and down as if she can't stay calm for a minute.

"That sounds good." Hannah and Lena laugh as they answer at the same time.

Getting into the cars, we head back up the road to get lunch. This road on the South Shore, called Snake Road as that is the shape of it is very dangerous at high speeds as there are cliffs off to one side and the West Bluff on the other.

Chapter Fourteen

"Table for four," Lena says to the hostess, taking over as we all expected she would.

"We should rent a campsite tonight," I spill out once we are all seated. "We can hike up to the doorway today and perhaps we will be able to go back to the lake in 1891 a bit longer than last time."

"Yeah, we should. We have to work tomorrow afternoon anyway," Hannah eagerly replies. "We are all eager to go back. It just seems to be the most enjoyable place we have ever been. The last time we were there, we had to leave early because of work so we didn't get to see as much."

"Then it's settled. We will go back out to the lake, rent our campsite, set up camp and hike back up there."

Nicola manages to devise a plan and we all nod in agreement.

"We will have to rent on the North Shore. You want to hike the East Bluff from there?" I ask, making sure we don't waste time.

"Yes, I think that will be perfect," Lena answers, much to our surprise.

"Hey, Hannah and I were discussing earlier about how Arthur and his family seemed to just take us in not wondering where we came from. What do you guys make of that?" I ask Lena and Nicola.

"It seems as though this type of magic has happened before, and they have seen it or have heard about it happening," Lena says, taking a bite of her food.

"I don't think they really seemed surprised so I will agree with Lena here." Nicola takes the easy way out of answering the question.

"Perhaps we can find out," I say, thinking that there would be some stories told amongst those that are there all the time.

"Yeah, let's go back, visit others and see the lake in that era," Hannah says. "Perhaps someone will mention this type of magic happening before like Lena said.

Dropping Lena off at home to get her mom's permission and pack, the rest of us head home to pack as well. Hannah and I head to my house first. We all have decided to use lawn chairs to sleep on but will bring a tent for changing our clothes. It's too hot to sleep in the tent so we may as well enjoy the great outdoors.

"So, do you think the warden will let Lena out for an entire day and over night?" Hannah asks as I am gathering my stuff from my room.

"Probably not," I answer as I stuff my sleeping bag with my pillow. "I am sure Lena will have a long list of chores to finish. Okay, so I am all set. Let's go!"

Hannah and I head out for her house. Hopefully, her dad is awake so I can help her pack.

"Alright, I am going inside and get my stuff as fast and quiet as I can," Hannah says with a finger to her lips. I let out a small snicker as she closes the door quietly. Ten minutes later, she is back, and we are ready to head over to Nicola's.

"Nic! You here?" I holler as Hannah and I just walk in without knocking. It's like our home away from home.

"Upstairs," Nicola hollers back as we hit the top step.

"Let's load your stuff and hopefully we don't have to wait long for Lena." Hannah grabs Nicola's sleeping bag and heads back down the stairs and out to the car.

"Well, there it is. Lena is ready," I say as I read her text and send a reply that we are on our way.

"That was fast," Nicola says as the three of us pile out the door and jump in the car.

"I don't think she had many chores to finish but I am sure she has to make supper for the terribles," Hannah adds as we all laugh to her reference to Lena's sisters.

Pulling up to Lena's, we wait patiently, and I send a text letting Lena know we are outside.

"Here she comes," I say as I pull open the door and head for the trunk so she can load her stuff.

"All set?" I ask.

"Yep, but I need to make a stop first." We all look at each other.

"Okay, where to?" Hannah asks curiously, since she is driving today.

"Pizza Hut."

"Lena, we already had lunch." Nicola smirks, clearly thinking that Lena must be starving again.

"Oh, it's not for me. I am going to prepay for supper to be delivered to my sisters. Then, I will have completed all my chores," Lena matter-of-factly shares without so much as a twitch.

"So, Lena, what did your mom say when you asked about the overnight and all-day thing?" I ask, just dying to hear this. Everyone in the car is silent. Not even the radio is turned up. We all don't want to miss a thing.

"Well, at first she was chewing me out because I had plans for the afternoon and I still had chores to finish." Lena pauses. We sit there thinking the same thing, would she just finish and kill the suspense that is lingering.

"I went to my room, decided to pack my stuff, and then finished my chores. I did all that, grabbed my stuff and here I am." Calmly, Lena lets out the nervous breath she had been holding in from the moment she decided to just leave.

"So, you didn't get permission?" I ask, wanting to clarify what I am thinking happened.

"Exactly! I decided that I was going no matter the consequences," Lena answers my question just as I thought. *Bold,* is all I can think.

"Lena, you didn't ask if you could go nor tell your mom where you are going?" Nicola is still trying to piece it all together.

"That's right. I have had just about enough, and I wasn't going to let her ruin one more day, at least not today," Lena says as her voice starts to quiver as she begins to realize what she did.

"Well, here we are, Pizza Hut. Want us to come in with you?" Hannah asks as we pull into the lot. Hannah hasn't said much the whole way over, so I am wondering what her turning wheels are thinking.

"No, I can do this. Be right back."

"Wow! I can't believe Lena did that," Hannah finally lets out as Lena walks across the parking lot to the door.

"I know. Sometimes though, people just bust. There is only so much one can take," I share, showing concern for Lena. As Lena makes her way back to the car, the three of us change the subject quickly.

"All right let's get to the lake before the day gets away from us," Lena says as she straps on her seatbelt.

****

"Here you are, ladies, site two-forty-four at the Northern Lights Campground." We pay for our campsite and set off down the road to set up camp.

"Okay, let's set up the tent here and just set all our supplies in the tent while we are gone." Lena has already composed a to-do list in the car; taking charge like she does so well. Not one of us has said anything more about her just going without permission from the warden.

"Let's keep all wood and perishables in the trunk of the car. We don't want them stolen while we are gone," Lena commands as we all do as we are told.

"Let's hit the trail!" Nicola exclaims with her arms flailing. Sometimes we wonder where she gets her energy.

Taking the trail from the campground toward the lake, we turn onto the road just before the railroad tracks. This road takes us back to where you can launch a boat and where the dog area is. Just before going up that hill, we turn left and head down the east bluff trail.

The trail up the East Bluff from the North Shore is not as steep as those on the South Shore. Walking down the scree path, we come to a fork. To the right is the actual trail up to where Elephant Cave and Rock are located and the rest of the trail that will take us to Devils Doorway.

Straight ahead of us is a scree path much wider than the other. This is an emergency road for emergency crews, and it is also known as the East Bluff Woods Trail. We can hike it if we want but the scree makes conversation almost obsolete and is a bit difficult to navigate going uphill.

Taking the trail to the right, not one of us is saying a word. We are quietly mulling over Lena's boldness to take on her mom.

"Whoo hoo!" Nicola lets out a loud whoop, which makes the rest of us jump.

"Nic, really?" the three of us say as we each take turns laying a nice punch on her arm. We stop to catch our breath from Nicola scaring the crap out of us.

Laughing, we are grateful for the break in silence even if it scared us. Nicola always seems to have a way of breaking the ice.

"Sorry, guys," Nicola says as if that will make up for it.

"It's okay, Nic. We needed a holler out at least once today," I tell her as we get back on the trail. Hikers are a minimum this afternoon as the humidity has finally reached its worst.

Stopping at Elephant Rock, we take turns sitting out on the rocks that are furthest out and overlook the lake. The scene from this view is beautiful, the slight calm of the water with a haze lingering just above from

150

the humidity. The haze looks as though it were afraid to touch the water the way it seems to dance along.

Heading back to the main trail, we stop to spray on mosquito spray as this trail lingers through mostly woods and the humidity causes them to hang out waiting to steal your blood. This trail is not smooth as it winds along but it's still beautiful. Another view of how the lake can surprise me.

"So, do you think we will get to go through the doorway today?" Lena wants to know as she seems more at home there and her persona changes for the better.

"I hope so. It will be nice to stay and visit longer and see more," Hannah says. We almost forgot she was back there. She has been unusually quiet for most of the hike.

"Lena, how is Nate?" Nicola snickers picking up the conversation from before lunch.

"Nate is good, very nice and easy to talk to. I haven't laughed so much. I was beginning to think I had forgotten how, except with you guys." Stunned, not one of us says a word. Lena just shared something private that I am sure she never thought she would ever do.

"Who are you and what have you done with Lena?" Hannah asks in her most serious voice and straight face. I bust out laughing which seems to catch everyone too. We all keep pace on the trail, laughing. Finally, reaching a straight away on the trail and after killing just about every mosquito out here, we reach the top.

"Nate is a nice guy. He seems to really like you, Lena. You look happy when you talk of him." I keep the conversation between us as we take our rest at the top and take in the view.

"He is very nice. Oh, Rin, I really wish I hadn't been so mean to him before."

"Lena, everything happens for a reason and I am sure he won't hold it against you. He is probably glad that you are talking to him now."

"You know, we never really discussed it. We just talked like we had always talked and easily."

I stand there taking in the view, listening to Lena. Finally, she is getting all of what I have been trying to share with her. Although, I also think our jaunt back in time has helped her as well. Her tough girl persona is slowly weakening.

"Hey, guys, look!" Hannah and Nicola holler to us as we get up from our perch to see what all the commotion is about. The guys that invited us to their campfire the other night are kayaking across the lake. They look funny, as they seem to be tipping each other over. So much for smooth . . . kayaking.

We all laugh as our anticipation increases upon reaching Devil's Doorway. Our last visit gave us a small insight to what the lake looked like long before our time.

"This time I hope we can see more and experience more," I tell the others as we each climb up into the doorway grateful that we are alone momentarily.

"Me too!" Nicola chimes in.

"And not only to see one side of the lake, but perhaps all of it," Hannah adds knowing that we may not have that kind of time.

"Let's just get there first," matter-of-fact Lena says.

Chapter Fifteen

Standing in the doorway, we all take one step and back we are. The humidity is just as stifling as back at home. Taking Balanced Rock Trail down, we stop to view the rock that gives this trail its name. From the steps, we cannot touch it unless we venture off the trail. In our time, we can touch it, sit by it, and take pictures next to it. Very different set up.

Reaching the bottom, we head off toward the railroad tracks. We pass the Kirk house and farm fields to the wooden bridge over to the tracks.

Taking our time, we walk past the beautiful Kirkland Hotel.

"I just can't get over how gorgeous the lake is with all these hotels and orchards," Hannah whispers quietly.

"I love the little cottages lined up along the lake with their own beaches." I sigh.

"Well, we have toured the Kirkland Hotel already. Let's keep walking toward our favorite beach spot and see all the other changes," Lena suggests and not one of us is complaining.

Detouring off the main path, we decide to go closer to the water for a better view of the lake. A boat pier comes into view.

"That's the Kirk pier." We all turn at the sound of a familiar voice.

"Afternoon ladies," Arthur says as he tips his hat.

"Hello," the four of us reply not expecting to see Arthur again.

"Enjoy your day." We watch as Arthur wanders down the path.

"Look!" Nicola points to the edge of the East Bluff along the water. "Are those cows in the water?" We all look and there is a small watering hole kept separate with a fence.

"Those cattle must come from the Kirkland house," I add, just assuming and hoping that I am right. We all stand along the shore, watching people getting into boats and paddling on. So much to see and enjoy, it just seems that there was always something to do and people were doing.

Heading back up to the main path, we walk further finally arriving at another hotel. Entering the Lakeview Hotel, a small sign shows the rates to stay. The rates are two dollars per day and eight to twelve dollars per week.

The first level consists of an office, music room, a bar and dance hall. On the second level, there is a kitchen, dining hall and sleeping rooms. The third level consists of more sleeping rooms.

Stepping back outside, we turn and take a long look at the Lakeview Hotel. The second and third levels show balconies wrapping all the way around the building with a staircase leading to ground level.

"This hotel seems to be more formal than the Kirkland," Hannah says quietly. We walk around to the back and there are more orchards, vineyards and farmland.

"Look!" Hannah points out the two barns located behind the Lakeview Hotel. In our time, this is all covered with parking stalls, picnic shelters and trees.

"Not only is the lake filled with hotels, vineyards, guests, but life. People actually live here," Lena says.

"Let's see if the Lakeview Hotel has cottages as well. Maybe one is available, and we can rent it for the night," I suggest, thinking it would be great to stay here longer.

"Let's do it," Hannah and Nicola agree.

Re-entering the Lakeview Hotel, we find that, indeed, they do have cottages but much to our dismay, they are all full.

"That's okay," I tell the clerk and head back out the door.

"Let's go back down to the Kirkland and see if they have one," Lena suggests.

Taking our time down the path, we greet each person we pass with big smiles. Glancing out across the lake, I see the same four cottages tucked in against the West Bluff.

My eyes continue looking up. "What is that?"

"Looks like a tower of some kind and that there." Lena points just south of the tower. "Looks to be a . . . house?"

"There is no house on the West Bluff."

Nicola snickers and snorts. "Apparently, there was at one time."

"Come on, let's get a cottage and then we can do some more investigating," Hannah says, eager to get moving.

Arriving at the Kirkland, we all stop again in awe of seeing it again.

"And to think that there is just grass and a bird mound where this building sits in our time," I tell them as we start up the walk toward the porch.

"Afternoon, ladies. How may I help you?" the clerk asks politely.

"Are one of your cottages available for this evening?" I ask in a more polite manner than I normally speak.

"Yes, we have one left for the evening. That will be two dollars. Your cottage is number one. Take the path to the right. Best fish caught from that pier this side of the lake."

I take two dollars from the small delicate bag that hangs with a strap from my wrist. The dollar bills look funny. They aren't the same as in our time. Perhaps they changed when we changed clothes walking through the doorway.

The clerk fills us in on where we are going and all the while he seems enamored by Hannah. We quickly say thank you and head back outside.

"He couldn't stop looking at you, Hannah," Nicola teases as we head down the path toward our cottage.

"Did you see the money?" I ask, wondering how it could just change like that. "I remember reading about them, and they were called treasury notes with a rounded red seal and red serial numbers. Edward M. Stanton's picture is on the one-dollar bill and were nicknamed Stanton." I share a bit of research with everyone.

162

"Yes, I did. It must have changed when we passed through the doorway. It was larger than what we use," Lena replies, guessing the same as I did about when the money had made its change.

"What is that building?" Hannah avoids the comments about the clerk and our discussion of the money. "I don't recall seeing that building from the doorway."

"Well, let's check out our cottage then we can walk down and see what it is," Lena says as we make our way up the path. We take a quick look inside. Sitting down, we try to figure out what to do next. We have plenty of time before its dark out.

"Let's check that building first."

"I noticed a boat heading over to the southwest corner of the lake. I wonder what is over there and is there a path to get there?" I know my curiosity is getting the better of me.

"Rin, I saw the same thing. I think we should see if there is a path over there." Lena seems much more relaxed again.

"You don't want to catch one of the boats over?" Hannah inquires since it's so humid out and we are not used to wearing all these clothes.

A knock at the door interrupts our thoughts and conversation.

"Hello, ladies. I heard that you had checked in."

"Hello, Arthur, so good of you to stop over," I say as I open the screen door and invite him in.

As he steps through the door, he removes his straw boater hat and gives each of us a nod.

"I just stopped in to say hello and check that everything is good here. You ladies have the best cottage at the lake."

"Thank you, Arthur. We were just discussing taking a walk and seeing more of the scenery."

"Perfect weather for that, ladies. Enjoy your walk. I will not keep you any longer," he says, placing his hat back on his head and walks down the path.

"That was sweet of him to stop by," Nicola says as she waves her hand feverishly out the door to the silhouette that has gone around the bend. "Let's go!"

"Let's find a place we can refill this water jug before we start. I bet we can find some at the Kirkland," Lena suggests in a quiet voice. Taking our time, we stop at the end of the dock to check out the lake. A boat steers away from a few docks south of us. Leaning as far as I can, I am trying to read the name on the side.

"What does that say?"

"That's the Minnewauken, a steamboat that will take you to the north end of the lake if you choose to go." We all look at each other then back to the polite woman.

"Thank you, ma'am."

"We have time to visit the North Shore, let's finish the South Shore first. We don't want to rush." I believe we will have more opportunities to come again.

Getting back on the main path, we head toward the bird mound to the building we noticed earlier that seems to be parked right on the lake.

Reaching the building, we stand and view it. When it was built, they started it on the hill and as they continued, they added a rock foundation to make up for the lack of hill so it could be built out toward the lake.

The walls were built with wood siding and the same goes for the roof. Upon arriving, closer, we see that a porch seems to continue around the building.

"Excuse me," I address the girl sitting quietly in the hammock staring at us with much curiosity.

"Yes, how may I help you?"

"What is this building?" I ask, not sure if it's a home or business.

"This is the Kirk Wine Cellar. We sell wines as well as making it right here," the girl explains to us, giving a slight hand gesture toward the lower level.

Taking the girl's cue, we head down the small hill toward the front. Stopping for a moment, we take in the view of the lake. Turning back toward the wine cellar, we head toward the door. Opening the door, the cold, dampness of the air hits as we walk in.

"Now this is a place I could stay in all day," Hannah says, referencing the cool air compared to the humidity outside and let's not forget the long dresses we are wearing. Looking around, we see barrels lined up along one wall and the further we walk in, it gets a bit darker and cooler.

The room is filled with shelves that are made like the shape of a diamond. Stacked in each diamond, a few bottles of wine and cider lay on their sides. Each bottle is made of glass and closed with a cork just like in our time.

"This is great," Lena whispers, like she is in a library. "You would never have thought this when we are at the lake in our time."

"Let's go up to the top and look around the store," I suggest needing to get out of the cold and damp cellar.

We head back outside, stopping to view the beauty of the lake once again and how busy it seems to be this late in the day. Climbing back up the hill, we turn to the door and enter the store. Once inside, it is cooler, like the downstairs. There are small diamond shaped shelves holding bottles of wine and cider lining the walls, and a small refrigerator, shaped like a cabinet with windows, keeps cheese cold for sampling with the wine tasting.

To participate in the wine and cheese tasting, you must participate in a rowing regatta and win a race, paddling across the lake and back. Anyone who out-paddles Mr. Kirkland, gets to participate in the tasting.

This we find out from the store clerk after I ask for a sample taste. The four of us look at each other and decide that we will think about it. Not one of us is athletic enough to paddle anything anywhere.

"We could give it a try," Nicola suggests. "What's the worst that could happen? We tip over?" She laughs.

"Exactly!" Lena exclaims in her drill sergeant voice. One we haven't heard in quite a while.

Heading back toward the Kirkland, we decide to fill our water jugs and head to the southwest corner of the lake on foot. Taking our time, we pass the Lakeview and its many cottages along the lake. Stopping at our favorite beach spot, there really isn't a large beach here like in our day. The water is higher, but it is still our favorite place.

Chapter Sixteen

Walking along the footpath, we pass a house. In our time, this house does not exist, and there is a wooden footbridge that runs in front of this very spot over to a sidewalk.

"I wonder whose house that is," Lena says, as we pass by keeping good time in this heat.

"It sure is big and has to have the best spot and view at the lake," I add. "Let's be sure to ask Arthur the next time we see him."

Finally reaching the road, I see it's not much of a road, compared to our time.

"There is no way a car would fit on this," Nicola laughs.

"Pardon me, it's a footpath to Messenger shore. Most people come to Devils Lake by train even some locals from Gem City," a fisherman answers, sitting along the rocks that line the lake.

"Thank you for sharing that. We would never have known."

"You're welcome. Enjoy your walk," he says politely, turning back to his fishing.

The four of us continue walking in silence, lost in our own thought of all this difference at the lake. I think about how much I would have enjoyed this type of living. There is no hustle and bustle. No massive reason to make tons of money, although, the people with the hotels do not lack the visitors. Which I supposed is good. People recognize the beauty of the lake and enjoy the quiet as well as the fun.

"Look at that!" Hannah exclaims as she has noticed all the cottages lining the south bluff. They all seem to be built right into it. In our time, there are parking spaces where these cottages use to be.

Continuing along what we call South Shore Road, we glance toward the north end and can see a lot of activity.

"We will have to visit the north end soon," I tell everyone, curious to know what is going on over there.

Finally, reaching Messenger Shore, we stop and rest for a moment after our long walk. Here at Messenger Shore stands a hotel and another building. As we venture along, we see people playing croquet and horseshoes. Everyone greets us with smiles and hellos.

"It's hard to believe how nice everyone is here," Hannah says since in our time people are too busy to be this nice.

"I know. It's nice to receive a smile back when you give one," Lena says.

"Let's head over to the hotel and take a look around; find out more," I tell them as Nicola just nods her head in agreement.

Reaching the hotel, we look at its façade. It's a two-level building built flat on the ground with a porch around, two stories, bedrooms and a parlor on the ground floor. Plain in view, but still a wonder as in our time there sits a parking lot for vehicles and boat trailers.

Next to the hotel is a pavilion that serves as a dining hall, kitchen and an entertainment house for those guests staying at this end of the lake.

174

Coming back to the large yard in front of the hotel, we face the lake. A boat sits along the dock with a paddlewheel on the back.

"Let's go down there," Nicola says, pointing at the dock.

We all head off through the marshy grass toward the dock. Tied there is a paddlewheel boat called Alvah.

"Now that's a different name."

"Oh, look a refreshment stand. How convenient," Nicola hollers out and skips over to see what they have. The refreshment stand also has bathing suits and oars for the two boats. All along the shoreline there are many more boats and docks.

People begin to gather on the large lawn out in front of the hotel and the shade from the large trees are very inviting.

"Let's go over and find a place to relax," Lena suggests, hoping the shade will help in keeping us somewhat cool from the ever-rising humidity.

"Hello. May we join you?" I ask a small family sitting in the shade enjoying a few snacks and refreshments.

"Yes, you may," a small boy replies.

"Thank you." The four of us sit for a while listening to chatter amongst everyone. It seems that the marshy area has hay growing there and is harvested to feed their horses.

"Farmers Picnic Days, I wonder what that is?" Hannah asks in a whisper.

"It's a day where people go to the Kirkland and there is singing, volleyball and baseball, different races and tug of war," the small boy informs us as he continues to enjoy his snacks.

"Thank you," I reply.

"That sounds like fun," Nicola says. "We should come back for that." We all look at each other knowing that we never know when we can come back again.

From Messenger Shore, we can see the South Shore and how different the lake looks. There is no road coming down the bluff in an "s" shape. There is a dirt path mostly from horses, but not very wide. Apparently, cars are not allowed down the path yet.

The lack of trees along the South Shore makes for a different appreciation. Life is what lives at the lake. Not just during the warm months, but year-round.

"I wonder how they survive in the winter here?" Lena asks curiously.

"I guess we will have to ask and find out," I suggest.

"Winter here at the lake is cold but we do not lack fun. There are toboggans, which we take to the North Shore for the run," the small boy sitting next to us says. "There is also a snow train that brings visitors for the small ski slope at the north end. We also ice skate right out on the lake."

"And life here at the lake?" Hannah asks him politely.

"It's not as busy as the summer months but there is still plenty to do here. Activities change some with the weather, but we prepare for the changes and it's simple." This boy, who seems way beyond his years, finishes his explanation with a smile.

"Thank you for sharing," I say.

We all sit and relax, just enjoying the views and sounds of the boats running on the lake. We will need to head back to our cottage before it gets dark.

Taking the same route back to the South Shore, not one of us is talking. No one argued about walking back rather than taking a boat even after it was offered. Arriving back to our rented cottage, we take in some of the lake from the boat dock just out the door.

"I think we should take the boat over there to the west bluff and hike it." Lena is quite eager to check out the cottage located at the top. "It sure is different to see it there."

"Do we have enough time to do that? I don't want to get stuck there in the dark." I know it's not safe to hike at night.

"I am with Rin on this," Hannah agrees. "Let's go over there in the morning and hike it."

"Oh, all right," Lena says all defeated for once. "Let's see what events they have brewing at the Kirkland tonight." Lena suggests gaining her composure from being defeated.

Taking the path up to the Kirkland, we arrive on the grounds to a view of beautiful lanterns lit along the path to the pavilion and the uplifting, enlightening and swing-like feel of music flowing from the pavilion was that of any we had never heard.

Happily, we enter the pavilion watching as the other visitors and locals dance gaily to the music. The four of us stand along the wall, clapping and tapping our feet to this beat. Arthur swings by and offers a quick wave of his hand. Circling back around the dance floor, he grabs Nicola's hand and out on the floor they go.

Arthur takes each of us out for a dance. It's the most fun we have ever had and all the while we wish dances back home were like this.

Stepping outside, Arthur joins us for a bit of cool air that has swept along the lake. The sky is clear and is littered with stars you could almost reach up and touch.

"Thank you, Arthur, for giving us a night to remember," I say.

"I think we will head off to our cottage and get some rest," Lena says as Arthur turns and heads back into the dance.

"Thank you, ladies," he says as he tips his hat before closing the door.

We make our way along the path back to our cottage.

"I have never had so much fun." Nicola yawns and stretches her hands over her head.

"Me either," Hannah agrees, yawning as well.

"Let's get some rest. We have a long hike up to the doorway tomorrow and back to our regular campsite." Lena gets us back to reality. "Goodnight." The peacefulness of the lake makes it easy to fall asleep.

Chapter Seventeen

Sitting quietly in the early morning, I am enjoying the beauty of the lake. I notice many people scurrying about. Something seems out of sorts for this serene time.

"Ms. Rin, you are awake early," Arthur says in a rushed voice.

"Yes, I enjoy the lake this way. Quiet, although, everyone seems out of sorts and up early."

"Yes, there has been an accident. I have to go now but I will be back to fill you in." Just as quickly as he stops Arthur is gone.

"An accident?" I say aloud. "I wonder what kind of accident. It's so peaceful here. I wouldn't have thought that were possible."

"Talking to yourself again, Rin?" Lena asks as she steps outside.

"No. Arthur stopped by rather quickly. He said there was an accident."

"Here, at the lake?" Lena asks.

It isn't all uncommon for there to be an accident back home at the lake. Someone was always rock climbing without proper gear and falling or a hiker standing to close to the edge or even a drowning.

"I guess it's possible in this time as in ours," Lena says.

"I guess I just never thought much of it here," I say, thoughtful. "Arthur said he would be back to let us know."

"Let us know what?" Nicola asks, as they have finally crawled out of bed.

"There has been an accident here at the lake. He will fill us in when he gets back," Lena explains.

"Gosh, I hope everyone is okay," Nicola says with a worried look on her face.

"It will be fine. Let's find some breakfast and maybe take a walk," I suggest.

After breakfast, I stretch as we walk out into the sunlight.

"We should walk through the vineyard and orchards," Hannah suggests.

"And then head over to the West Bluff to hike up to that cottage," Lena says with anticipation. "I cannot wait to see that."

"I agree. I think we should just head straight there. What do you think Hannah, save the vineyards and orchards for when we get back?" I ask to make sure we will have time to get there and hike that bluff and get back to the South Shore. "We do have work this afternoon."

"Sure, why not," Hannah answers without any argument.

"Let's fill our water jugs again and get moving." Lena grabs her jug and heads for the Kirkland.

"Wait for me," Nicola finally chimes in.

Reaching the Kirkland, we fill our water jugs and decide we better find out if there is a boat we can take over to the West Bluff from here.

"I will go in and see if we can get a boat over. I am sure the one I have seen on the lake can take us." Lena heads up the stairs and into the pavilion before we can respond.

"Guess we will just wait here," I say as the three of us standoff under a tree to try keeping cool.

"The Capitola comes by every half hour at the big dock." Lena comes back with the information on the boat.

Isn't that the same dock that Arthur was fixing earlier today?" Hannah asks as we make our way down the path toward the pier.

"Look, look!" Nicola screeches, pointing to the pier. "The boat . . . what's it called? It is just about to pull up to the pier, we better hurry."

"Watch for any broken boards," I holler to her just as she misses a good board and ends up with one foot in the hole between boards and into the water.

"OW!" Nicola yells out as she collects herself and pulls her left leg out of the water and hole.

"Sit down," I say. "Let's look at the scrape and fix it up."

"Can't we get on the boat first?" Lena whines impatiently, not wanting to wait another half hour. "But the boat is right there, and we could get on, fix Nicola up in the few minutes to the North Shore."

"Lena does make a good point, Rin," Hannah says carefully as I send her a scowl.

"Fine. Come on, Nicola. Let's get you on the boat so I can fix up that leg." I finally give in and help Nicola on the boat.

The Capitola is at least four feet long and twelve feet wide. Its whistle sends out quite a shrill as it begins to pull away from the pier.

"Holy crap!" Lena screams, slapping her hands over her ears. "That scared the crap out of me." I start laughing so hard my stomach starts to hurt.

"Why are you laughing?" Lena puts one hand on each hip, looking at me with the most pissed off face I have ever seen.

I try to slow my breathing so I can explain that I knew about the whistle. I remember reading about it when I was researching the lake after our first visit to 1891.

"I am laughing because I knew about the whistle before it blew," I explain as I try to keep from laughing again.

"And you didn't think to tell us this before?" Hannah asks with a small snicker.

The whistle blowing didn't seem to affect the rest of us like it did Lena. I think because we were focused on Nicola's scrape.

"Calm down, Lena," I say as I finally catch my breath and turn back to Nicola's leg. "Let's get this cleaned up and bandaged. It's not a bad scrape."

"Oh crap!" Lena says like the world is about to end.

"Now what?" I ask, annoyed that she can't seem to just sit down and enjoy the boat ride.

"Look – we aren't headed to the north shore." Lena points to Messenger Shore with a scowl on her face.

"That's okay. Now we will get to see all the lake from a different perspective," Hannah says, trying to lighten the mood.

"This is great! Hopefully, the boat will go along the West Bluff and we can see the South Shore from there," Nicola says as I finish up bandaging her scraped leg.

"Just relax, Lena. Try to enjoy the boat ride with the view," I say to smooth things over with the two of us.

The Capitola comes to a brief stop in front of the pier along Messenger Creek to allow some passengers to get off and just a couple get on the boat.

"Lena, here comes the whi . . ."

The whistle blows again just before I can warn Lena that it will be sounding off as the boat pushes away from the pier.

Clasping her hands over her ears, Lena shouts, "I really wish they would give a warning!"

"I tried to warn you, but it sounded before I could get all the words out." I sit idly by laughing in a quiet tone, so she doesn't hear me.

The Capitola begins the voyage to the North Shore by passing along the west bluff where there are three more cottages with their own piers.

"I never noticed those before," Nicola says, pointing at the cottages.

"Yes, they are the same ones we see in our time, but I think they are updated," I say as I try to see the cottage atop the west bluff. "I can't even see that cottage up there. Definitely a different view from here."

The Capitola comes along in front of the North Shore Chateau and heads toward the pier near the Cliff House and Annex.

"Check out that house set back up against the hill." Hannah points out across what we know as picnic area in our time to see a house with barn and cattle.

"That is the Claude house," a fellow passenger tells us. "It is owned by Louis J. Claude."

"Thank you. We haven't been to the North Shore before." I politely thank the passenger for the information as the four of us look on and imagine our beach and picnic area where this farm currently sits.

The Capitola reaches the pier at the Cliff House and parks there for a time. The four of us get off the boat and head toward the monstrous hotel.

"Look at the size of it. There are two parts that seem to be connected," Nicola says with delight.

"I wish Arthur was here. He could help us navigate this shore much like he did the South Shore,"

Lena says, sounding as though she is hesitant to be venturing out on our own.

"I doubt Arthur would be much help. I think he mainly stays on the South Shore. Let's go inside and see if someone can help us."

We walk from the pier toward the railroad tracks. There is a flag stop there for the train and a boardwalk that leads right up to the Cliff House. Walking up the steps, we head into the front door.

"Good afternoon, ladies. How may I help?" a kind gentleman says to us as we make our way toward the desk he stands behind.

"Good afternoon. Do you have any rooms for the evening?" Lena asks in the politest voice I have ever heard.

"Yes, we do. The rate is two dollars and fifty cents per day or ten dollars per week," the polite clerk says.

"Thank you. May we take a tour of the hotel?" I ask, curious about what this hotel has due to its large size. My previous research showed that this hotel was the more elegant hotel at the lake compared to the ones on the South Shore.

"Yes, feel free to tour and my name is William and I would be happy to answer any questions you may have."

"Thank you. We will be back," I reply as the four of us go back outside to view the hotel.

The hotel consists of two buildings: The Cliff House and the Annex. The Cliff House has verandahs and galleries extending around the entire building.

"Let's go back inside and have a look around," Nicola says as she walks back up the stairs onto the porch. The rest of us follow.

The Cliff House has a very spacious dining room with a great view of the lake. The maximum capacity for visitors to eat in the dining room is 200 people but only those adorned in the proper attire. Men wear suits and dinner dresses for women.

As we walk through out the hotel, we notice there is a telegraph, ticket and baggage office, a post office, a grocery store, a barber shop, a billiard room, and the first bowling alley in the area.

We stop back at the post office where we saw William. "Excuse me, William," I interrupt him as he is sorting mail.

"Yes, how may I help you?"

"With the Cliff House being so elegant and large, why was there a need for the Annex?" I ask, using that research to aide in my questions.

"The Cliff House was once called the Minnewauken and when it changed owners it became known as the Cliff House and was quite popular. At that time, the Cliff House could only house about 200 people in the 63 rooms. So, the Annex was added to accommodate the many visitors which added another 30 rooms and now we can accommodate up to 400 people."

"Wow. That's a lot of people," Nicola says, not really realizing how many visitors the lake actually gets each summer.

"Yes, it is," William answers with a chuckle that makes his belly move up and down.

"Are there other accommodations if someone did not want to stay at the Cliff House or if it is full for the night?" Hannah asks, anticipating my next question.

"Yes, there are a few family cottages, a log cabin and even camping available."

"Thank you, William. We will let you get back to your work," I tell him as I start towards the door and back outside onto the verandah.

"Anytime. If you have more questions, I will be right here," he replies as he turns back to sorting the mail.

"I wonder where those cottages are located?" Lena says, thinking those might be a great place to stay as opposed to the large hotel or annex.

"Good question, Lena. Let's walk around some more and see if maybe we can find them without having to bother William again."

"Let's not wander around too much. We will never get up on the West Bluff if we diddle too long." Lena is excited to get up to the top and see that cottage.

"Okay, okay," Hannah says to get Lena to calm down. As we walk the path it passes in front of a barn and house.

"We will have to come back and visit this shore a bit longer," I say as we pass by the house and finally reach a trail that seems to be the same as ours going up the West Bluff.

Chapter Eighteen

"Let's break for a few minutes before we head up. Isn't this exciting?" Lena seems less like a drill sergeant now and more like a kid at Christmas.

"My research showed that this cottage wasn't here long. Not nearly as long as the others we have seen," I share with everyone.

"I wonder why," Nicola says as we start up the west bluff trail.

"There must have been something in your research Rin that stated what happened," Hannah says what the others are wondering.

"Yes, I am trying to recall exactly what it was though. I will keep pulling at my thoughts as we make our way up."

"Let's rest when we reach a flat spot at the top. This trail isn't nearly as bad as Potholes is," Lena says with a small hint of drill sergeant coming out in her voice.

I keep trying to recall why this cottage wasn't here as long as the others as I bring up the rear of our hiking party. Seems to me that there was a death of some kind, but I cannot recall whose.

We stop at the top for a quick rest and to take in the views of the lake from here. "Everything looks so different than our view at home." Hannah points out from the edge. "All the cottages and hotels and lack of parking lot space. It's just so beautiful here."

"Yes, it is," Nicola adds.

"Okay, let's continue our hike and find that cottage," Lena commands and for a small bit she is back to her normal self.

"Wha . . . what is that?" Lena stops and is looking up toward the sky.

"That's a tower," I answer, recalling some of the research I did. "I think they were planning to put a telescope in the top part."

"That is cool. I wonder if the telescope is up there," Nicola says bouncing around. We all laugh as she is showing her natural antsy pants self.

"It is definitely cool," Hannah agrees with Nicola.

"Look! There's the cottage right on the edge of the bluff." Lena points and starts running toward it.

"Lena watch ou . . ." I holler to her just as she face plants it on the trail.

"Ouch! Where did that rock come from?" Lena sits up rubbing her chin.

"Your chin is gashed pretty good. Anything else scraped up?" I ask as I am looking for something, we can use to help stop the bleeding on her chin.

Lena sits there pulling up her dress to assess the situation on her knees.

"Knees look good. Thank goodness for all the layers from this dress." She laughs some.

"How about your elbows?" She pulls up the sleeves, revealing small scrapes, but nothing compared to her chin.

"Good, so we just have your chin to bandage up. I sure hope you don't need stitches."

"What? It's that bad?" Lena starts to panic as if there wouldn't be a doctor here to patch her up.

"I am sure there is a doctor here and if not, we can take the train into Gem City and find a doctor who can give a better idea as to how bad it is." No need to panic.

"Okay. That sounds good."

"Hannah, hand me a water jug so I can clean out this scrape." I take the water jug and pour it over Lena's chin. "Scrape doesn't really look too bad. All we have is this old cloth from the doorway. Just hold it there and that should keep it from bleeding anymore." Finishing up on Lena's chin, she gets back on her feet and we continue down the trail toward the cottage.

The cottage is quite large with two floors. There seems to be perhaps an observation floor at the top. We are unsure because we did not tour this cottage. Just looked at it from the trail. We wander around to another area that shows some building being done.

Looks as though some more cottages will be built like a little neighborhood.

"If I recall my research, this was supposed to be a resort area which included lots, parks, and even a hotel," I share what I finally remembered.

"Wow!" Lena says just standing in awe at the site where this resort looks to be underway.

"It doesn't happen though," I tell them. "As I remember, the owner of this cottage on the edge of the bluff died of typhoid fever and it wasn't finished. People were too afraid." I can't believe how much I am remembering from what I read.

"Great stuff to know," Hannah says. "I think it's a good thing that this was never finished."

"I agree. Let's look around and then we better get back to the South Shore so we can hike up to the doorway and get to work." Lena pulls the work card.

Nicola has been quiet. "Nic, are you okay?" I ask her.

"I am all good, Rin. Just taking it all in." She is usually all bouncy.

"I want to come back," Lena says as we make our way back down the trail toward the North Shore. "I want to see the North Shore more."

"Lena, you know we can try," Hannah tells Lena with an unsure look on her face. Hannah has been the one who worries that we will get stuck here in 1891.

"Hannah's right, Lena. We can try but let's get home and off to work," I agree with Hannah.

"Yeah, who would want to miss checking out those hotels here on the North Shore." Nicola points down the trail as we finally reach the bottom.

Chapter Nineteen

We finally reach the South Shore and start our journey back toward the doorway. Reaching Balanced Rock Trail, we begin our hike to the top and back to the doorway. Standing at the doorway, Lena's rush is much slower because she doesn't want to leave. None of us do.

"Okay, up we go," Hannah says as she helps us up into the doorway.

"Now you, Hannah," Nicola says as she and I pull Hannah up into the doorway.

Lena stands at the edge not sure she is ready to cross back into our time.

"Okay, Lena, we have to go back. No matter how much we would rather stay, we have responsibilities to get to," I say matter-of-factly and in a drill sergeant way.

Lena takes one step through the doorway and nothing happens. She is still dressed in the long dress and lace up boots.

"Now what?" She turns to me with a scowl on her face.

"Well, it took all four of us at the same time to cross over to this time when we arrived, maybe we need to try that again," I answer her calmly.

The four of us stand together and take each other's hand, taking a step through the doorway and again nothing happens. We are still in 1891.

"We didn't go back," Lena says with a small touch of excitement.

"Let's try it again. Nicola, you count like you did when we got here."

"Okay," Nicola answers as we all take each other's hands again. "1-2-3," Nicola counts out and we all take a step through the doorway and to no avail, we are still in 1891.

Sitting down in the doorway, hanging my legs over the side, I try to figure out what exactly happened here. Are we stuck here for good? We have come across this question before but that was the very first time and we have always been able to get back through.

"What do you think, Rin?" Hannah asks as Lena and Nicola look at me with hopeful eyes that I may have an answer.

"I don't know," I say. "I truly do not know why we can't get back."

"Well, I don't mind that we can't get back," Lena says. "I wanted to spend more time here and now we can. Let's take advantage of it."

Hannah, Nicola and I look at Lena like she has totally lost her mind.

"Lena, what if we can never get back?" Nicola says, getting a little bit wound up. "I don't want to be stuck here forever. I like it here, but I like it at home, too."

"Yeah, Lena. We have a job and our families. They will all be wondering what happened to us when we don't show up for work today."

"I don't care. I have had enough of my mother treating me like Cinderella in a real-life story. I want to be able to say what I am going to do and when," Lena says with her arms flailing around.

Grabbing Lena's arm, I notice that her bracelet is missing. "Everyone check for your bracelets," I tell them. "Nicola, what did you say you made these out of?" I ask her with a suspicion.

"Leather strands I found in a box in the attic. Why?"

"This leather looks old, very old," I say as I take my bracelet off and begin to look it over.

"What are you thinking, Rin?" Hannah asks while looking at my bracelet as well.

"When we all arrived here yesterday, we were all wearing our bracelets. Today, Lena is missing hers," I say. "I think that these bracelets maybe the key to being able to pass from 1891, home and back."

"Rin, it's just old leather I found in a box. What really makes you think that these are allowing us to time travel through the doorway?" Nicola says matter-of-factly.

"I'm not sure but every time we have ever been to the doorway and climbed up and crossed over to the west side of it, we never crossed into a different era. But the first time we crossed over to 1891, we were all wearing these as you gave them to us on our hike up here that day," I explain.

"So, what you are thinking is that because I don't have mine, we can't get back without all of them?" Lena asks.

"I knew it. I just knew we would get stuck here with no way home." Hannah starts to panic.

"Exactly, Lena. Calm down, Hannah. We need to decide what to do next." I try to get everyone to calm down.

"We find Lena's bracelet that's what we do!"

Hannah exclaims.

Chapter Twenty

Disappointed that we couldn't get back home, we climb down out of the doorway once again still wearing the long dresses and lace up boots.

"Where should we start first?" Hannah asks eagerly.

"Let's check the cottage we stayed in first," Lena suggests.

"We should probably make sure that it isn't re-rented already," I say so we don't go barging in on people.

Making our way down Balanced Rock Trail, I wonder again why Nicola has been so quiet. I make a mental note to check-in with her when we reach the bottom.

Reaching the bottom, I suggest we take a rest to catch our breath before heading to the Kirkland. Hiking in these long dresses is more of a chore than we are used to.

"Nic, are you okay?" I seek Nicola out to ensure she is doing good.

"Yes. I am thinking about the bracelets and wondering about the leather they are made from. I didn't notice anything different about the box the leather was in and if it could provide some clue."

"We can look at it when we get back," I tell Nicola. "Let's find Lena's bracelet first and get home."

Back across the Kirkland bridge we make our way to the Kirkland to find out if the cottage we stayed in is empty.

"I'll just go in and ask," I tell Lena, Hannah and Nicola. I make my way up the steps and enter the Kirkland. Stopping in the entry way and look around before making my way to the desk. "Excuse me," I say to the clerk.

"How can I help you?" he asks.

"Yes, I am wondering if the cottage we stayed in last evening is empty," I ask the clerk, telling him it's the one closest to the wine cellar and the one with the best fishing.

"Yes, it is empty. Can I help you find something?"

"If we could just have the key for a few minutes. We are looking for a leather bracelet one of us lost," I explain.

"Sure, I can give you the key. No one has cleaned it yet," the clerk answers as he hands me the key. I take the key and make my way back outside; I flash the key to the others.

"Let's go!" I say, heading down the path toward the cottage.

Reaching the cottage, we all enter and start looking everywhere: under beds, under blankets and pillows, and in all the cabinets. No bracelet.

"It's not here," Hannah says, starting to panic.

"This is only our first stop," I say, trying to calm her down. "We have more places to check. I did find that old cloth we found near the doorway," I say, putting the cloth in my little coin purse.

Stepping outside, we run into Arthur. "Hi, Arthur," I say as we walk to the main path.

"Afternoon, ladies. How are you today?"

"We are doing good. Arthur, what happened earlier when everyone was rushing about?" Lena asks, knowing we all are thinking the same.

"A rowboat had floated ashore last night. It contained personal items of a man and a woman. The couple haven't been found yet. There is an investigation started as to who they are and such," Arthur explains.

"How awful," Lena manages to say.

"We haven't concluded to what may have happened," Arthur explains. "Many of their personal effects were still in the boat along with a Kodak Brownie Box camera. The film will be developed and hopefully we can find out where they had been staying."

"Well, let's all be positive that they turn up alive," Hannah says, which eases the tension some.

"Yes, we can all hope for the best," Arthur says, tipping his hat. "Good day ladies."

"Good day Arthur," I answer as he leaves us.

"I hope everything turns out for the best for that couple," Lena says.

"Okay, where do we look next," Nicola asks.

"Well, let's check the Capitola," Hannah suggests. "We did take it to the North Shore."

We reach the dock that the Capitola pick-up tourists from and we happen to be lucky that the boat is there waiting.

"Let me ask if we can take a quick look around." Lena takes control realizing the importance of the bracelets. The rest of us wait patiently on the dock.

"Let's go. Lena is waving us over," Nicola says carefully walking down the dock. We all climb aboard and start looking near the same spot we had been sitting earlier that day.

"It's not here either," Lena says as we all make our way back to the dock.

"Okay, after riding the Capitola we were on the North Shore and hiked up the West Bluff. We don't really have time to do that again, do we?" Hannah asks, knowing that it is possible Lena could have lost her bracelet on that trail.

"You know what?" I ask. "We spent the evening before at the pavilion and dancing, remember?"

"We didn't look there," Nicola says. "Let's go!"

Chapter Twenty - One

After spending all day searching for Lena's bracelet, we finally found it at the Kirkland pavilion where we spent the prior evening dancing and enjoying the festivities.

"I am so glad we found Lena's bracelet," Nicola says as we bounce along the trail that leads up to Balanced Rock.

"Me too! Because if I am right, we need it to get back home." I reiterate how I feel about the significance the bracelets are to our time travel.

"Let's just get to the doorway and get back home," Hannah anxiously says. "I feared we would get stuck here and I truly hope that you are right Rin about these bracelets.

Reaching Devil's Doorway again we each climb up into it to take that step home.

"Check!" Nicola says after checking to make sure we each have our bracelets.

"Okay let's go home." Hannah is eager to get home. We all are even though we love it in 1891. We each take our turn walking through the doorway as our clothing changes from the long dresses to shorts and t-shirts again.

"Rin, I guess you were right about the bracelets," Lena says.

"Yes, but I am still not sure how or why they worked," I answer back still puzzled by everything. I'm puzzled by Arthur and his family accepting us so easily, puzzled by our bracelets being key to our time travel, puzzled by the display of rock stacks out in the water, puzzled by the voices whispering along the trail from Potholes to Devil's Doorway and even puzzled by the old cloth we found at the doorway. My mind is racing as we all climb down from the doorway.

"We are home," Hannah says with a huge sigh of relief.

"It's late. We better get back to the car and head for home." Lena starts off onto the trail heading to the North Shore. Finally getting to the campsite we rented, we pack up the car.

"Well, that's everything. I guess I will drop you all off at home and see you tomorrow?"

"Hopefully," Lena adds, anticipating she could be grounded or set on house arrest for being gone so long.

"Thanks, Hannah," Nicola says as she heads for her house.

"Do you think they'll get into trouble?" Hannah asks me as we drive toward my house.

"Lena, maybe, but Nicola won't. Tiffany will try to discipline her but Nic will just ignore her.

"What about you?"

"I doubt anyone will notice I am late. Too many other worries to be concerned with," I answer, knowing that no one really pays much attention to what I do. Oh, I follow the rules completely, but I don't think it would matter. "Do you think your parents have been worried?" I ask Hannah, not really knowing her parents that well.

"No, I am guessing they figure we all were working late. Lena will probably be the only one to get in trouble."

***

Arriving home, I manage to get to my room without any argument from my parents. I am still trying to figure out if in fact the bracelets were the key. I think seeing the box the leather came in might help. I think to myself while getting ready for bed and putting that old cloth in a safe place. Time to get some rest since we have to work at noon tomorrow.

Chapter Twenty - Two

Lying in bed wide awake, my mind is starting to churn about what the cause was for us getting stuck in 1891. I pause for a minute and realize – it's quiet. There's no television blaring or any arguments going on.

Heading for the stairs, I take my time walking up the first set to the landing and peek around the corner, listening for signs of life – it's quiet.

I take the last four steps up and make it to the kitchen. Walking around upstairs I realize I am pretty much alone. Marie's keys are on the counter with a note giving me permission to use her car for work today. She has the night off and doesn't need it.

Maybe I was missed, and they did notice I wasn't home early. I think to myself as I go back to my room to get ready to take a shower. I call Hannah after my shower and suggest we all meet at Nicola's.

"Sounds good. Do you want me to pick up Lena?" she asks.

"No, I have Marie's car so I will call Lena and pick her up. You go ahead and call Nicola and tell her we're coming over." I set a plan in motion for the morning. I want to see that box the leather came in and I want to know how much trouble anyone go into last night.

"Hey, ready to go?" I ask Lena from the deck outside her house.

"Yep." Lena bounds out the door and down the stairs before I realize she is out the door.

"Off to Nicola's!" I say loudly. Lena laughs.

***

"Hey, Nic, you home?" I holler as Lean and just walk in the house.

"Downstairs."

"Hannah here yet?"

"Not yet. She said she will be here in about ten minutes." Nicola turns on some music as we all take a seat.

"Hey, you guys," Hannah hollers as she bounces down the stairs and takes a seat on the couch.

"So, did any of you get into trouble for getting in late last night?" I ask because I want to know if it was just as weird for them as it was for me.

"My parents just figured we ended up working late," Hannah shares just as she thought they would think.

"Tiffany tried to pull the mom card, but I just blew her off and went to my room."

"What about you, Rin?"

"Pretty much the same. It was as if I were an afterthought until I woke this morning, and no one was home except Marie who was sleeping and left me her car keys."

"Lena?" We are all waiting to hear if she got into trouble like always seemed too.

"No. I didn't. My mom was still home and was waiting when I walked in the door. I thought for sure I would get into a ton of trouble because I didn't ask permission to go camping and for coming in late. Nothing. She just hugged me and told me she loved me. Then this morning I mentioned having to work at noon and that we all wanted to meet up at Nicola's before

work and if I could go as soon as my chores were done."
We didn't even consider that Lena's mom would have
been worried at all. She usually hands out punishment
to Lena like the plague.

"Wow. I guess we all thought you would be
grounded or something," I say after listening intently.

"I thought the same, Rin, but here I am. I didn't
even have any chores to do. My mom said that my
sisters could start earning their keep by doing some
chores."

"That's great, Lena," Hannah says. "It's about
time your sisters help you out."

"It is but I am wondering if it is the calm before
the storm," Lena says, anticipating that this could just be
temporary, and her mom will go back to the old ways.

"Well, I am glad we all got back from 1891 safe and that none of us got into any trouble," I share. "Nicola, what you got there?"

"This is the box that leather came in for our bracelets. I pulled it out last night when I got home. You were so adamant Rin that the bracelets had to be the key to our time travel, I wanted to have a look," Nicola explains, holding the box.

Nicola hands the box to me carefully. I can see that it is quite old and fragile. The top has a logo, but I can't see the name as it has faded quite a bit with time.

"What do you think, Rin?" Nicola asks.

"It's hard to tell since the name and logo are so faded," I answer, unsure that this box could be over one hundred and twenty-five years old. It is an old box but not sure it's that old.

We each take turns holding the box and looking inside at the remaining leather. Handing it back to Nicola, she gets up and takes it to the counter until she goes upstairs later.

"Thanks, Nicola, for getting the box out," I say.

"No problem. Like I said, I was just as curious about it."

"So, Rin, if you don't think that it could be the leather bracelets, what do you think it could be?" Hannah asks, curious now that we have possibly ruled out the bracelets.

"I'm not sure. Perhaps we just went through a portal that has been opened somehow," I answer, still not completely sold that it isn't the bracelets.

"But then how did it not open for us when we tried to get back yesterday morning?" Lena asks, getting involved in the conversation.

"Good question and I truly do not have an answer for that," I answer her.

"Well, let's get ready for work and think more on it. If we are off tomorrow, we should try to go back," Lena says.

"And get stuck again? No way!" Hannah sarcastically says because she was the one who warned us that we could get stuck and we did.

The rest of us laugh and head out to the cars for work. Our night goes quick and we find that we are off tomorrow so I guess we will at least hike. Not sure we will try to go through the doorway again so soon. We all leave work and head for home agreeing to meet up at

our favorite beach in the morning.

Chapter Twenty - Three

"It's gorgeous out here this morning," I say in almost a whisper as the four of us stand on the beach taking in the view.

"This is great for a Monday," Lena says, feeling liberated that she didn't have to do a ton of chores this morning and was not told to be home at any specific time.

"It is but I am betting the water is quite cold this morning," Hannah says, dipping her toes in the water. "Yep. Just as I thought, too cold."

"So, let's hike Potholes trail. It feels as if we haven't hiked that trail forever." Nicola bounces up and down picking up the pace and heading off down the trail ahead of us.

"Okay! Let's go!" the rest of us chime in and try to catch up with Nicola.

"I remember now how hard it is to hike this trail," I say as I try to catch my breath. "I couldn't imagine hiking it with those long dresses like they wear in 1891."

"Let's rest here." Lena picks a nice spot for us to rest and take in the morning view. It is busier than usual probably due to the cooler temperature in the mornings. We rested for quite a while which is unusual for Lena to allow us, but I think this new found experience with her mom has lightened her up some.

"We are almost to the top. Let's keep going and rest when we get up there," Hannah says, starting up the trail again. We pass through the puzzle piece again and I take a few minutes to enjoy it. It seems forever since I have seen it and it's my favorite part of this trail.

Reaching the top, we hike a bit down the trail and find the nearest bench to take another rest.

"What do you think?" Lena asks what we are all thinking. "Do we try to go back?"

"We could try I guess." Hannah surprises us with her response since she was so against it afraid to get stuck again.

"Let's do it!" Nicola says, once again bouncing down the trail toward the doorway. We all follow and manage to keep up this time.

"Do we all have our bracelets on?" I ask making sure that we all are wearing them and hoping I am right about them being the key to our time travel.

We finally reach the doorway and of course we all stand and take in the view of the lake. It never changes but always feels like the first time.

"Alright, Hannah, lets help up Nicola." Lena starts giving out orders and none of us tease her of sounding like a drill sergeant. We just let her relish the moment.

Lena goes up next and I follow. Hannah comes up last since she is taller than the rest of us. We stop and enjoy the moment of being in 2018 before we make a move to venture once again into 1891.

"Okay, let's do this," I say to get us moving. Standing in the doorway is a small space for four people. We walk through the doorway to find that we are still in 2018.

"What happened? We are all wearing our bracelets. Why didn't we go back?" Lena starts to freak out as if life depended on going back in time.

"I don't get it," I say, trying to figure out why we didn't go back.

"Maybe it isn't the bracelets. It could be something else," Nicola says quietly, trying to get Lena to calm down some.

"Nicola could be right, but what could it be?" Hannah says as we all finally sit down on the west side of the doorway dangling our feet over the edge.

"I don't know." We had the bracelets on when we went through on Friday and we couldn't get back on Saturday because one was missing. I run this scenario through my head trying to figure out what we missed. Lena finally calmed down and we all just sat there quietly. I am sure we all were thinking the same thing about how it worked before and trying to decide why it wouldn't work now.

"I'm hungry." Leave it to Nicola to bring us all back to reality.

"Me too," Lena finally says. "Let's go down to the South Shore store and get a hotdog.

We help each other down from the doorway and our mood is dreary on a nice, hot, humid and sunny day. We make our way back down to Potholes trail and begin our decent. It's quiet on the way down and we didn't even stop to rest. We pick up our hotdogs and head to our favorite beach and sit quietly eating.

"Let's swim the rest of the day," Lena suggests. We all think that is a great idea since the disappointment of not going back in time hasn't cleared the air.

"I'll get the floats," Hannah says, since we keep the bulk of our swim gear in the trunk of her car. The rest of us head down to the beach and pick a spot to layout our towels. Hannah brings down the floats and sunscreen and we all lather up before heading out into the water.

"Hannah, water is warmer now," Nicola teases, since Hannah stuck her toes in earlier and it was cold. We all know that it really isn't warmer, we are all hot and sweaty.

Our disappointment stays with us as we all decide that we should just go home rather than staying longer or hanging out together. We each make our way home knowing we will see each other at work tomorrow.

Made in the USA
Middletown, DE
02 May 2021